FOREVER HIS

IN THE DARK, BOOK ONE

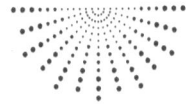

VIOLET HAZE

STOKED PUBLISHING HOUSE

Forever His ©2015, 2019 by Violet Haze

This is a work of fiction. Names, characters, places, and incidents are the product of the author's imagination or are used fictitiously. Any resemblance to actual persons, living or dead, events, or locales is entirely coincidental.

Cover Design from Designs by Dana
Stoked Publishing House
ISBN-13: 978-0-9992261-5-5

SIMONE

"Don't waver."

I kneel on the tiled floor with my arms behind me and my back straight as I command my body not to falter. This position serves two purposes: it juts my breasts out as the gifts they are thought of being, and indicates my subservience since such a position was demanded of me by Master.

And I've been holding it for a good twenty minutes now. Although it's a guess because I can't see anything in the surrounding darkness, and haven't been afforded a way to tell time since I arrived here.

Where is here? Fuck if I know.

Either way, every minute feels like forever, and numbness in my knees is fast approaching. But I can't move; won't move. He has to find me this way, or there are consequences.

I wish I could say I'm afraid of them, but I can't. I've never experienced them because I've done everything asked of me since the beginning. I didn't fight.

Not that I didn't want to fight; I just knew there was no point.

And I suppose I'm afraid to find out what the consequences are exactly, which is why I won't move even as the tingling in my heels amplifies. I bite my lip to keep from making any noise in reaction to the feelings, and hope he arrives soon, as I was told he would when informed I should prepare for his visit.

I'm in the dark and have been since I was put into this room — the only exception is when I'm cleaned and even then I'm blindfolded. Naked all the time and chained up as well except when he's here. Fighting would only cause me pain and other than the kind of pain Master gives when fucking me, I'm not interested in being hurt.

My thoughts go to the collar around my neck. It's rare for it to cross my mind anymore, but when alone, I stroke it and run my hands around it. There's no way to get it off, but hoping I'll suddenly find a way to remove it anyway is a regular desire.

It's steel, smooth, and if I had to guess, permanently locked. When I touch it and move my fingers around it, I feel a sliver of a space and there, a little hole. I've no doubt it's a tiny screw and the device to remove it would have to be very tiny — probably a tiny key or something.

When Master first locked the collar around my neck, I cried. It felt heavy and cold and uncomfortable to sleep in. At rest, it met my collarbones, and getting used to it had been my biggest challenge. He would pull on it and there was no give — if I didn't move, it would dig into my skin, and I'd move because I had no other option.

He only had to tug on it hard once when I wouldn't move to prove his point, and I've never resisted again. It was also the last time I cried; after that, I simply gave up any hope of leaving this place.

Lost in thought, the touch of his hand on my shoulder makes me jump, wobbling for a moment in my stance before using all my willpower to make sure I don't fall, and I hear him chuckle.

The sound is, as always, muffled. I don't know if he wears a mask or what, but he never speaks once we've begun kissing and fucking, and I suspect it's because he doesn't want me to recognize him by voice, ever.

"Good girl." He trails his hand up my neck to the top of my head, before flattening his palm against the top and sliding it down my hair. "I've kept you waiting and you've done exactly as you should."

"Yes, Master."

"You may sit down and relax. I know your feet must be numb."

"Yes, Master." I suck in a breath as I move to sit down, but swallow my cry of discomfort as my feet and legs instantly burst back to life, pins and needles shooting through every inch. "Thank you, Master."

The tile is cold on my ass, but damn does it feel good. And once I'm comfortable, I slide my hands back behind me and clasp them together, as I know he expects.

I sense him walk away, now that I'm not inside my mind, and for the millionth time, wonder what he looks like. I've never seen him. I have just felt him in me and around me. I'm not allowed to touch him either. He always keeps my hands tied together or away from my body and his, no matter what position I'm in.

I'm not sure where he walks off to. The room is pitch black. There are no windows, and I'm not sure when the last time I saw daylight was. I'm sure any light now would hurt my eyes so bad, and I'm glad he doesn't torture me that way. He stays consistent and I find comfort in what he's given me.

"Master?"

My voice is meek, wincing because I know he likes it when I'm strong, but I've never asked him a question without being prompted first. I don't know why I chose now to do it.

"Have I given you permission to speak, Cara?"

"N-no, Master. Sorry, Master." My tongue feels heavy in my mouth as I swallow at the name he gave me, knowing he's walking toward me even as I apologize, and hoping I'm not about to find out what the punishments are.

He stops in front of me, the soft fabric of his pants brushing the left side of my face with how close he is. "Are you able to stand?"

I know it's not a question he wants an answer to. He wants me to rise, and so without using my hands, I get on my knees before rising to my feet, continuing to face the same way.

"It's been a few days, Cara, hasn't it? I've neglected you."

"No, Master," I respond in an instant, knowing the correct way to answer by heart. "I'm happy with any attention you wish to give — or not give — me, Master."

He moves behind me, and when his hand comes up to move my hair to one side, I let out a sigh of contentment and relief. His hands slide down my arms, and when they reach my waist, one moves around my side until he's wrapped it around me. Stepping close, I feel his cock through his pants, resting in the crack of my ass.

My body responds to his touch, no effort necessary. His mere presence is now enough to send my body into full-blown sex mode. My nipples tighten on their own, my pussy wet and ready without even being touched, eager to take him inside and be fucked raw.

Hard and fast, or however he wants it. I'm his slut and nothing more. He's made it very clear I only have a name because he's given me one; without that, I'd only be a nameless vessel for his desire.

"You're gorgeous, Cara. So fucking gorgeous." He removes his hands, and while I make sure to keep our bodies touching, I feel his hands between our bodies. The sound of him unbuckling his belt makes me want to moan, a desire I repress as I hear it slipping through the hoops, followed by him slapping it against his legs. "I'm going to miss you when you're gone."

"G-gone, Master? What do you mean?"

He doesn't speak, but before I know what he's doing, he steps away and the belt hits me on the upper thighs.

I'm unable to stop the howl of pain and surprise, because this is the first time he's ever hit me with the belt, and I'm not sure why he's doing it. I can't even move because I don't know where I can go in this room, and I keep my hands behind my back while standing in the position he left me in.

"You're the perfect slave." He doesn't answer my question as he walks around me, clothes brushing against my hot skin as he stays close as possible. "I expected a fight, but you're smarter than that, aren't you? You've done nothing except please me from the beginning, and I only wish you were mine to keep. But you're not. And soon, you'll go home."

"Why—?"

I'm cut off with another hit of the belt, and my howl is louder this time as I dance on my feet, another hit coming before I can even recover. Tears spring to my eyes, soon trailing down my cheeks as he hits me over and over again, moving the belt up and down from my thighs to my ass and back again. I dance in place, knowing if I move from my spot it will probably get worse.

"Please, Master," I wail. "Please, stop."

"Are you telling me what to do?" He raises his voice, and I know I've shocked him with my disobedience, which he confirms by hitting me again. Really hard. "I know you're not telling me what to do, Cara."

"I—I don't understand." I sob through my tears, stilling my movements even as my shoulders shake, my whole back side burning and tingling. "W-why are you mad at me, Master?"

I hear the belt drop to the floor in response, the buckle clinking against it, seconds before Master's hand wraps in my hair and guides me over to the bed.

"Bend over," he bites out as he releases me, his clothes rustling behind me as I do what he says, placing my left cheek against the mattress as taught while keeping my hands behind my back. "Hands above your head."

I slide them up, palms down, covering one with the other in the way he prefers and wait. I don't dare speak again, but all sorts of thoughts rush through my mind.

I'm going home? Why? I know I should be happy, but I'm confused. Why was I even here in the first place if he was going to let me go? What am I missing? And if it upsets him, why is he letting me go?

He smacks my ass and I stiffen, jarred out of my thoughts once more, as he puts his hand in my hair once again. Tugging it back, I lift my head even as I force my body to stay put as he desires, and a whimper of mixed pleasure and pain escapes.

"I'm going to fuck you right now, Cara. You want my cock pounding your pussy, don't you?"

"Yes, Master." I lick my dry lips, the very idea of him fucking me making my pussy clench with anticipation. "I want you to fuck me any way you like, Master."

"I always fuck you any way I like. And you like being my slut as much as I like you as my slut, yes?"

"Yes, Master." My words emerge on a sob of desires as he slides his cock up and down between my pussy lips, and I move my ass in an encouraging manner, trying to get him to give me what we both want. "I'm your slut, Master, and I love your cock."

With no further warning, he rams his cock into my pussy, all the way, until the tip is pushing against my cervix and I'm grasping the sheets in my fists. My moan is loud as I feel every inch of him. He fills me and stretches me and pushes me to my limits with his cock alone.

He pounds into me, yanking harder and harder on my hair until my neck is burning with the stretching sensation, my nipples rubbing against the sheets underneath me in a way that has pleasure skipping through me at a rapid pace, and my cries grow louder and louder.

"Oh god. Oh god Master, please may I come?"

"Don't you fucking dare, Cara. You know you're not allowed."

"Please, Master," I beg, desperate to let go around him while he's inside me, so desperate I clench my pussy muscles around him as I sob harder. "Please let me come."

He doesn't answer me. Instead, he leans over my body, covering my back as he slowly releases my hair. I know better than to move though; I keep my head in place where he last held it and he buries himself to the hilt before stopping his movements. His hand slips around my throat, sliding his fingers to caress under my chin before following the path down to my collar, and sliding his hand around until he's gripping the back.

I whimper as he draws it toward him, until it's digging into the front of my throat, partially blocking my airway, and all I can focus on is the blood throbbing there. I can't move as he's holding me hostage, restricting my breathing enough to make me feel it.

He's not hurting me, thought, and withdraws his cock to the edge before plunging back in with such force as to make me gasp. I'm feeling lightheaded, his cock relentless, and when he speaks I have to force myself to pay attention even as he fucks me with no mercy.

"I know you touch yourself when I'm not around, Cara. But you never get off do you?"

"No, Master." My words are whispered, the haziness in my mind taking over more and more, but I know I have to keep answering him no matter how I feel.

"Why, Cara? Why don't you get yourself off?"

"Because you told me not to, Master."

"Such a good listener." His voice is steady and I wonder how he can fuck me like he does, but never sound out of breath. "Such a good fucking slut. Do you think you deserve a reward for being such a great slut, Cara?"

I know he values my honesty, so answer as I have to. "N-no, Master. I only deserve what you think I deserve, Master."

He groans, releasing his hold on the collar, and I suck in a breath of desperate air as he grabs my hips and fucks me even faster. Then, one hand slips around and down between my legs, and I cry out the moment he touches my clit. He plays with it equal in pace to his fucking, and I am barely able to gasp out the appropriate request, but I do it.

"May I come for you, Master? I want to come around your cock."

"Fuck, yes. Come for me, *now*."

It's easy to do as he says on his command, because I'm hovering on the edge, and I fall off with his strong stroke. My pussy clenches around him, my long moan of pleasure spilling out my lips, as my orgasm rips through every fucking inch of my body and has me shaking.

He moans, long and loud as he grips me tight, his release following mine close. He collapses on top of me, but he doesn't touch and caress me like he did before. After a few moments, he moves away, leaving me bereft of his touch and warmth. I lower my head and body to the bed, seeking something, anything to comfort me.

And I don't know what it is that makes me so sure, but I know this is the end, and since it is, I speak freely.

"Why?"

It's all I ask, but I know he knows what I want. The rustling of him putting on his clothes stops and he walks close, resting one hand on the small of my back with sigh.

I wait, relishing in the little bit of connection I get from his touch, knowing how much I'll miss something I never knew I wanted or needed until I ended up in this predicament. I'm sure people would think I'm crazy to think such a thing, but it's true. And I'm not sure how I'll go back to the life I had before.

"You're not mine to keep," he answers in a whisper, his hand sliding up my back and down again until it rests on the small of it once again. "And you must go home now."

In that moment I realize two things: his voice isn't muffled, which is why he's whispering, and sick and twisted or not, I've fallen in love with a man whose face I haven't seen and whose name I don't know.

Within seconds, he's gone from the room, and from my life, leaving me to sob into a pillow, releasing all the emotions I'm not sure I'll ever be able to define.

2

SIMONE

I CAN'T SEE anything when I hear the door of the vehicle opening, and I'm lifted from inside before being set on my feet. I'm wearing clothes for the first time in what feels like forever, and the sensation of shoes on my feet has me itching to pull them off and walk barefoot already.

"Don't take the blindfold off until you hear a honk," Master says in his muffled yet gentle voice from behind me, his hands resting on my upper arms. "You're a little down the street from your house, and I've placed you in the direction you need to walk. Do not look back when you've taken off the blindfold. Got it?"

"Yes, Master. Thank you."

I feel him move my hair to the side and lean close to my ear. "Good girl. I wish you well. And keep your lovely fighting spirit, Cara. Never have I been more proud of a slave in my life, and I'm sorry to see you go."

It's only been a few hours, if that, since he told me I was going home, and as he stands behind me, I want to cry and beg for him to take me back with him. To not do this.

But I know he won't. He's made it clear he won't keep me.

So, I square my shoulders, holding back the tears clouding up my eyes, and nod. "I will." He removes his hands and I whimper, before remembering to ask, "Master, how long have I been gone?"

"Two months." The door shuts as I gasp, and I hear his opening and closing as he gets back inside the vehicle. "Goodbye, Cara."

The car drives away and I stand there, shaking as I lift my hands up to my face, poised to take the blindfold off at the honk which arrives after a few moments. I pull it off, continuing to do as he bid by not looking back, and noticing I'm only two houses down from where I lived before.

Well, where I live now, too. I guess.

I walk toward my house, and lift my gaze to the sky, where the sun is just rising as I let the tears slide silently down my cheeks. So many sensations I'm not used to after being in a quiet, dark room assault me, such as the purse I'm carrying, which is the same one I'd been using when taken and heavy on my arm. I reach inside and easily find my keys as I approach the front door of the house

I live in, and after a slight hesitation, slide the key into the lock.

Perhaps it's because of what I'd just gone through, but the moment I walk inside, I can tell something isn't right. I shut the door behind me, set down my purse and keys, then head up the steps as I call out, "Henry?"

When he doesn't answer, I walk faster, heading toward our room even as I try to stay quiet because I know he's probably sleeping. But when I open the door, my hands fly up to cover my mouth as I pause in the doorway, taking in the scene before me.

The room is trashed, with clothing, beer bottles, and god knows what else strewn across the floor. Henry, my high school sweetheart and husband of three years, is naked atop the blankets, his hands buried in some girls hair as she crouches between his legs, his cock in her mouth. His head is back, his eyes closed, as he moans long and loud before saying, "Oh yeah, baby, just like that."

I don't even think, the utter disgust and instant rage I feel tearing through me at the scene in front of my eyes, as I pick up the closest thing to me and throw it. Lucky for him, the vase my parents got us as a wedding gift misses his head, shattering on the wall behind the bed and raining down on him instead, along with the water and the flowers in it.

His eyes fly open as he says, "What the fuck?"

Then, when he sees me, they widen even further if that's possible and he shoves the girl away as he scrambles off the bed. "Simone? What the hell?"

"Don't even!" I scream, shaking a finger at him and then at the girl, and take a step back. "How dare you! Did you even call the cops to let them know I was missing?"

"Calm down," he says, holding his hands out with the palms down, lifting them up and down. "You weren't missing—"

His statement catches me off guard and I blink at him, not understanding why he's saying such a thing. "What the fuck do you mean? I've been gone two months!"

"Baby." His tone is soothing, speaking low as if I'm a wild animal about to attack, as he steps closer to me. "Don't you remember us talking about fantasies? You said you wanted the whole experience of being kidnapped and kept as a slave…?"

"Oh my god." I step forward and shove him, which he doesn't expect, and as he lands on his ass, snap, "You fucking idiot! I wanted us to experiment with it together, not be taken by a stranger and…and…Oh my god! How could you be so stupid?"

From the floor, Henry's face blanches as he realizes what he's done, and shakes his head. "Simone, I figured you would know. I didn't mean—"

"No." I back away, lifting my hands up and shaking my head. "I can't believe you…I…I'm leaving."

"Simone—"

"Shut up! We'll be divorcing. I'll send you the papers. You can…" I wave my hand around as tears fall steadily from my eyes now. "You can keep everything. I don't want anything, you fucking stupid asshole."

In a flash, he's up off the ground, holding me against his body, whispering, "Please Simone, I love you. Don't go."

"Let me go! You just had another woman's mouth on your cock."

"I was lonely. She was just someone to have sex with. I missed you. Please baby…"

"I said, let me go!" I shove him again and he drops his hands, eyes filled with a misery I ignore as I turn away.

Walking downstairs, I pick up my purse and my keys, then leave the house and never look back.

PREGNANT.

I stare down at the test, unable to believe my watery eyes, the word on the digital test clear as day.

"Fuck."

The word comes out a whisper as I place the test on the counter and bend over the toilet once more to puke, my stomach revolting in more ways than one as the enormity of the situation settles over me.

I remember my last period came right before I'd been taken.

It's been a whole month since I arrived at home and promptly walked back out.

That makes me roughly three months along.

God, three months pregnant with the child of a man I don't know; a man who'd been paid to act out a fantasy and instead, had committed a crime in reality. And from my perspective, it really fucks up everything because I fell in love with my captor only to find out he'd been paid, and probably did that sort of thing for so many others.

Sitting back on my heels, I bury my head in my hands.

What in the fucking world am I going to do?

The divorce papers have already been signed and filed. Because we both agreed, we don't even have to appear in court so that's a relief.

I'm living in a one room apartment a bit closer to the city than I lived with Henry, but I'll have to leave. I can't risk him seeing me, and I don't want to ever see his stupid fucking face again. I could still kill him for what he did, but I think his current misery of losing me is punishment enough because I'm sure he does love me in his own fucked up way.

And honestly, I didn't do anything about what he'd done because I didn't want to go through all the legal stuff. The man who did what my husband asked thought I wanted it; how could I possibly punish him for doing something he'd been told was okay? Maybe he would've stopped if I had fought, but I hadn't.

There's no way I could tell anyone I didn't fight. It hadn't been long before I'd been begging for what he gave me, and wanting it with every fiber of my being.

Shoving a hand through my hair, I stand up and mutter, "Fucking idiot."

This time, I'm talking about me, and making a final decision, I head to my room to start packing my stuff up so I can get the hell out of here and figure out where to go from this moment on.

Especially since it looks like I'll have a baby to take care of.

3

SIMONE

Ten months later…

"ASSHOLES."

Grumbling under my breath, I wipe off the table decorated with ketchup and salt, the utensils used for the impromptu artwork laying on the plate I placed on the tray. It's crazy how people have no respect for those who serve them, making such a disgusting mess in a public place, and not even being decent enough to leave a tip to compensate for the extra time I'll spend cleaning this shit up.

Why am I working at this place again?

Oh, right, because I'm a twenty-two year old recent divorcee with nothing beyond a high school diploma, along with being a single mother of a four month old, and I need to take care of both of us.

Fat fucking chance on the amount of money I make, which isn't a lot.

With a heavy sigh, I turn to clean the next table, only to discover a man still sits there. A quick glance at the clock confirms we've been closed fifteen minutes. And, wouldn't it figure the table is my last one, and I'm not allowed to ask a customer to leave. I have to wait.

Wait. As if I don't like getting off on time and getting home at a reasonable time to get some sleep so I can do all the things I need to do the next day before coming to work again.

I'm about to turn with the tray to wash what dishes I have when the man lifts his head from the paper he's reading and stares right at me, following that up with raising his arm and crooking a figure at me to indicate I should step closer.

I do, gazing at him the whole time, pasting a smile on my face as I stop a few inches from where he's sitting. "How may I help you, sir?"

He doesn't respond right away, his gaze intense as he flicks his eyes down my body, then drags them back up in what seems like slow motion. They linger at my feet for a few moments, his mouth turning down in a frown, and I have the insane urge to run and hide my ugly, raggedy shoes from his glittering gaze.

I know what he'll see as he moves upward: stockings on the edge of getting runs from the small damages here and there, a black work uniform skirt covered up a little by the apron but not enough to hide how old it's getting, and a white button up shirt that's definitely seen better days. And when his hazel eyes finally meet my dark brown ones, his mouth moves.

"Your feet must be killing you in those shoes."

I blink, not expecting those slightly accented words to come out of his mouth, wondering why he cares. I open my mouth, only to close it again as I figure out what I should say. I decide honesty is the best policy; I don't know why, though. Maybe it's something in his manner, as he seems disappointed in someone, but I also get the feeling that person isn't me.

"Yes, they are." I look down at them and grimace. "I need new ones."

He nods, holding up his coffee cup as I glance up at him again. "If you will get me another cup of coffee to go, I will get out of your way." The corner of his mouth quirks up in a rueful smile as they flick toward the clock, then back at me. "I did not realize how late it was, and here I am keeping you from doing your job."

"It's no problem at all. I'll be right back."

I hurry to the back with the tray, sitting it by the sink before turning to get him a cup of coffee to go. The other worker, Mel, scowls at me as I rush around, but I barely pay her any attention, walking back to the man within two minutes.

When I place the cup with a lid on it in front of him, he says, "Thank you."

"You're welcome. I hope you have a great evening, and come back soon."

"Oh, I will."

He says that as I turn around to walk away, but other than a quick smile toward him, I keep walking to the back and empty off the tray so I will be able to use it on his table. By the time I return to the dining room, he's gone, and a piece of paper tucked in between the salt and pepper shakers is the first thing I notice as I approach the table. Picking it up, my mouth falls open as three-hundred dollars falls out onto the table, which I leave laying there as I read what he wrote.

"$200 for you and $100 for the other girl. You two work hard and are underpaid, if the state of your shoes say anything. Buy yourself a new pair. Have a nice night, Simone."

I look for his name but don't see it as my eyes tear up from such an unexpected kindness. Then, I shove the note in my pocket and pick up the money, running to give Mel her share of the generous tip which will not only buy me a new pair of shoes, but pay my electricity before they turn it off.

At least I'll sleep a little easier tonight, even if the feeling of relief won't last long at all. I'm in a precarious position thanks to the events of the last year, but I'm thankful for any small act of kindness, and head home with my heart a little lighter at knowing there *are* nice people in this world.

THE MAN WHO LEFT THE GENEROUS TIP DIDN'T come back the next day. Or the day following.

Matter of fact, it's a week later, and he still hasn't come back.

Apparently, he didn't mean it when he said, 'I will' after I'd told him to come back soon. And I'm dumb for believing he would mean what he said; if I've learned nothing else in my whole life, it's that most people are full of shit.

However, with the money the man gave me, I was able to pay my electricity and buy two new work outfits, along with some new shoes. I've never been so fucking grateful for new shoes in my life, and for the last week, it's felt as if I were walking on air. Rick, my boss, was also pleased with my improved wardrobe.

So, I want to thank the man, but I can't do that if he doesn't come back. However, as each day passes by and he doesn't show, the less and less hope I have he'll ever return.

And maybe that's for the best. Fuck knows I don't have the best track record with men and staying away from them might be the best idea. I just wish I could convince my heart to follow my head in that area.

"Simone," Rick says with a hand on my shoulder to get my attention. "Thanks for all your hard work tonight and for staying to help. You may go home now. Mel and I will finish up."

"Oh, great. I'll see you tomorrow then."

He nods, walking away with a smile, and I clock out after getting my stuff from the back room. Stepping outside, I finish pulling on my gloves and pull out my cheap as it gets flip phone to keep in my hand while I walk home. Walking in the dark should make me nervous, but it doesn't. It's also the cheapest option since I don't live far and I've never had any trouble in all the time I've been working at the diner.

Turning to the left, I only take two steps before his voice rings out, causing me to stop walking abruptly and turn toward his voice with wide eyes.

"Please tell me you don't walk home this late in the dark by yourself every night." He pushes away from the wall of the restaurant with a slow, elegant grace I've only read about in books, his hands sliding with a casual motion into his pockets as he approaches. He halts about half a foot away from me, flashing me a smile which seems rather bright even with the streetlight shining above us. "Or, at least assure me someone is picking you up any moment now, and you simply wished to refrain from standing still while you await their arrival."

My first thought is, why does he care; the second, has he been waiting for me outside? He must've been, but why? Perhaps I should be afraid, yet I'm not, and I take advantage of the silence as he waits for my answer to pay attention to things I didn't last week. Such as his voice, which while refined had been friendly last week; tonight, it's clipped, his tone filled with obvious disapproval. And his height and build, wow. He looks like he could pick me up and squash me with little to no effort as I estimate him to be around six-four, which makes him almost a foot taller than me.

He's wearing a black suit, with a white button down underneath, and no tie, with his shaggy wavy brown hair making his look a little less civilized than the rest of his appearance tries to make him out to be. I get the feeling he's hardly civilized at all, and take an involuntary step back as I say the most stupid thing I can.

"You came back."

"I said I would, didn't I?" He lifts a brow with his response, staying right where he's at, and I breathe a little easier knowing he's not trying to intimidate me. Instead, he studies me, his eyes dropping to my feet before sliding up my body in the same slow, deliberate manner he used last week, and he smiles as he meets my gaze. "Much better."

"Thanks. I um…I'm glad you came back. I wanted to thank you. It was very kind and you didn't have to—"

"Simone." Hearing him cut me off by saying my name, something I forgot he knew from my name-tag, I suck in a breath, and he smiles. "Yes, I remember your name. And our world could do with a bit more kindness, don't you agree?"

Opening my mouth to agree, I'm stopped short by the sudden gust of cold wind, which has me shivering and realizing I'm standing on the sidewalk freezing my ass off.

"I've gotta go," I say, nodding in the direction I'm facing. "It's too cold to stand here to talk and I have to get home to my—" Stopping short of admitting I have a child, I give him a smile, and say, "Thanks again."

His lips compress as he realizes I'm not going to finish my previous sentence, then proffers his arm as he steps closer. "Let me walk with you. You should not be walking home in the dark all alone." When I hesitate in taking it, he lets out a soft laugh. "You could tell me no, but then I will just follow you anyway to make sure you get there safely. So, stop overthinking it, take my arm, and we can get you out of this cold."

In my head I'm thinking only an idiot would take his arm. Only an idiot would trust a man she doesn't know, even if he gave her a huge tip for simply being kind. Even if he seems so nice and I don't get the feeling like he wants to hurt me. But who am I kidding? I know I'm an idiot, and like he said, he would follow me anyway.

I don't have any other way to get home and my babysitter is a nice middle-aged woman who watches my son for free, but relies on me getting home by a certain time. And something tells me he's an intelligent man; if he really wants to find out where I live, he would without having to walk me home to get it.

"You are smart," he says with a chuckle, dropping his arm. "I can see your mind working. Suppose I should introduce myself if I expect you to let me walk you home. Isaac Toft."

He sticks out his hand as he says his name, and after a moment, I offer mine. He grips it and before I can even blink, he pulls until my body is against his, wrapping an arm around my waist to keep me steady.

"I would like you to trust me, even though you don't know me, Simone." He speaks softly, his mouth near my ear, as he releases my hand to clasp the back of my neck. "All I want to do is make sure you get home safely. I am not going to hurt you, and you are fucking freezing, so let's go, hm?"

Other than my boss putting his hand on my shoulder, no one has touched me since my husband on the day I came home, and my affection starved body responds to this man's touch with a staggering speed. It's fucked up how aroused I am right now in the face of his raw strength being so close to me, but I don't care. I can't help it. In his arms I'm tiny, and at my size, helpless to get away. Even more so by the fact I don't want to run even though my heart beats rapidly in a fear I can't mask, which is only because my son is at home and I'm all he has in this world, not because I'm trapped in this man's grasp.

I don't fear him. I feel almost...safe, and perhaps that alone should frighten me because all he's done is be kind to me once. Yet I know I don't fear him because it's just like everything else since those two months I spent in the dark: I don't fear anything. I know this probably makes me so messed up, but I've not been right mentally after that and I'm aware of that fact. I'm in love with a man I've never seen and I have a child with him; it couldn't get any more messed up than that at this point.

I realize I've not said anything when he pulls back to look down at me, and my arousal heightens, pooling between my legs so I have to squeeze them together as an obvious flame ignites in his eyes. I recognize the answering desire in the quickening of his breath, in the way his arm around me tightens an infinitesimal amount, matching the hand on the nape of my neck. And it's clear to me that if he backed me up against the wall and fucked me right now, I'd let him.

But I'm not that lucky as all he does is say, "Simone, let's get you home."

And I want to cry as he slides me down until my feet touch the ground and hooks my arm through his, keeping me close to his side as we start walking. He doesn't say anything else until we reach my door fifteen minutes later, where he waits for me to stick the key in the lock before caressing my cheek with his thumb to get my attention.

When I lift my head to look at him, he leans in while moving to cup my cheek in his hand, and presses a light kiss to my lips before pulling back, saying, "I will see you soon."

He turns and leaves without another word or a backward glance, and it's only when I'm inside with the cold locked outside that it registers in my mind that I never told him my address.

4

SIMONE

My son, Malik, sits in his stroller next to me at the library the next day while I'm on the computer. Lucky for me the weather reached the high sixties today and the library isn't far from my place because it's imperative I find out anything about this man I can. I don't know what I'll find, but with how he made me feel last night and how I want to get to know more even if it makes no sense, something is better than nothing.

But as I put in his name and hit search, there's not much more than nothing about Isaac Toft. It's clear after opening a few different pages that he's a notoriously mysterious and reserved man which accounts for the utter lack of information. The most well-known public facts are about how he was born in England to his English mother who was a nurse and his Danish father who was an eccentric and reclusive geneticist, and they moved to the US when Isaac was ten years old. He finished school, became a stockbroker, and then quit his job three years ago after a broken engagement to an actress, disappearing behind the thick walls of his private estate.

A property which is listed as being in a town an hour from here, and yet, he stands outside where I work and waits for me, then insists on walking me home? He knew the address and I'm sure he knows more about me than I'm aware of. So the question in my mind right now is, why? Why is he interested in me? Before last week, I knew nothing of him, and I'm sure I would remember if I met someone like him before. I've not known him for long, but I can say with certainty he's the kind of man one would find unforgettable, because he would make sure of it.

Malik lets out a giggle and I sign out of the computer before looking down to find him staring up at me, chewing on his hand as he wiggles his feet. He moves them faster when he notices my eyes on him, making baby noises, and giving me a big toothless grin which showcases his chubby cheeks. Even though it's been four months since he was born, I'm still amazed at how much he looks like me, which I'm pretty glad for honestly.

"You ready to go? Yeah, mama's ready to go too."

It's a quick walk back to the apartments, and a few minutes after I go inside and place my son down for a nap, there's a knock at the door.

Looking through the peephole, I see the babysitter Helen standing there holding something, and when I open the door she makes a displeased face as she holds up a light blue box.

"This came for you while you were out."

Taking the perfectly square box from her grasp, I hold it against my chest as I say, "Thanks for keeping it safe."

"Sure. Didn't come in the mail though. Some guy was knocking like crazy on your door and when I told him you weren't home, he said to make sure you got it and ran off." She clucks her tongue and takes a step back. "I dunno who you know, but he wasn't nice at all."

A glance down at the package shows it has no writing on it except the elegantly scrawled words "For Simone" and I instinctively sense it's from Isaac. "I don't know anybody really. Come in and tell me about him while I see what this is?"

I phrase it as a question but it's clear it's not a request as she glides past me into the living room. After closing the door, I join her and sit down in a chair, placing the box on my lap.

"He was a tall skinny man, drove a black car, dressed like an undertaker. You don't know anybody like that?"

"No." Lifting the lid off the box, the first thing I take out is the note inside. Setting it on the table, my hands return to the box and move aside the paper until I touch cloth and pull.

Both Helen and I release a gasp as a light blue shimmering floor length dress opens up. A few seconds later, she lets out a whistle. "Well honey, you gotta know somebody because that box is definitely for you."

"I…" Not even able to finish my sentence, she picks up the note and hands it to me with an expectant look. Opening it, I read it aloud. "Simone, I will pick you up at seven for dinner. Wear this. No arguments. Isaac."

For some reason, Helen laughs and when I cast a glance her way, she says with a shrug, "Guess you'll be needing me to watch the baby for the somebody you don't know."

"The guy you're talking about must be someone who works for Isaac or something. I dunno, I only met Isaac last week, and he walked me home last night."

"You gonna go or not?"

"I guess. What do you think I should do?" Since I don't have anyone else to ask, and she's the closest thing to a mother figure I've got, asking her for advice seems natural. "I'm out of my element here."

"Well, honey," she says as she stands up and walks to the door. "If there's one thing I've learned in my life, it's that you don't argue with a man who says no arguments about taking you out for dinner. I'll be back when it's almost time for you to go in case you need any help."

"That's it? That's all you have to offer?"

She turns back to wink at me, one hand on her hip, her amusement clear. "Honey, if you didn't want to go, you wouldn't have asked me what to do. So yeah, that's all I've got. Get ready. You've got two hours."

5

SIMONE

HELEN RETURNS at six forty-five after I've gotten a shower, put on the dress, and did my hair. She moves to take Malik from my arms, lifting him into the air as he giggles, and she smiles right back at him.

"He's fed and changed and ready for play."

"Of course he is! Helen's the fun one, ain't that right Malik? You tell mama bye, have a good time, and not to worry."

At that, I laugh and put an arm around her shoulder, giving her squeeze before releasing her. "Now, I never worry when he's with you Helen. I know he's in skilled and loving hands."

Kissing Malik on the cheek, I walk over to the door to grab my coat, and then slip into it. Grabbing my purse and keys, I turn to Helen and slip my phone into my pocket. "I haven't told him about Malik, so I'm going to stand outside the door."

She nods, giving me a soft smile. "Send me a message letting me know where you're going that way if you don't come back I know where to send the police."

Her innocent joke makes me straighten my back as I give her a sharp glance, knowing she has no idea what happened to me because if she did, she wouldn't say such a thing. All I say as I open the door is, "I will. See you when I get back."

Blowing Malik a farewell kiss, I step outside and just shut the door behind me when I hear footsteps. Turning around, I'm surprised to see the man Helen described earlier approaching.

"Miss Winston," he says with a bow as he stops at the top of the steps. "Mister Toft awaits you in the car."

"Who are you?"

He must not have expected the question because he blinks as if confused, and then gives a soft laugh. "I'm his driver, personal assistant, delivery boy, and many other things. My name is James Richards, but you may simply call me Jim. Shall we?"

"Um, will you tell me where we're going so I can send a message to my...friend? You know, safety first." I can't help the small smile I give back to him, some of it because he seems nice if a little nervous, and the rest because on the inside I'm thinking this safety rule doesn't make much sense if you think about it. After all, if someone is going to 'take me to dinner' only to kill me, they're hardly going to give anyone the right address. I'd say going out in general is a risk in that case, but I'll do what Helen asks anyway.

As for Jim, he nods and rattles off an address after I pull out my phone. Once it's sent to Helen I follow him to the car, putting my keys and phone inside my purse. I don't know what kind of car it is, but when he opens the door and I slip inside, it's clear it's an expensive one. It's dark out already and at first, I don't see Isaac inside the car which is probably closer to a limo in design. I've never been in one of those either but I think anyone who watches any TV knows what those are like interior-wise.

But then, his hand grabs mine and he pulls me down beside him, where I land with a squeak of surprise as Jim shuts the door behind me. Readjusting my position until I'm sitting correctly, I set my purse to the side of me while my eyes try to adjust to being able to see almost nothing. Not even the streetlights come through darkened windows of the vehicle all that well, which makes me frown and ask, "What's with the mystery?"

The car starts to move a moment later as Isaac's hand gives mine a gentle squeeze.

"No mystery," he says with what I would bet my life on is a dark chuckle. "I don't go out where I will be seen unless it cannot be helped."

"And yet you sat inside the well lit place I work at?"

"I took a one-time risk."

"Why?" When silence greets my question long enough it makes me uncomfortable, I change the topic. "Where are we going to eat?"

"Private dinner for two at my place."

I jerk my hand out of his, what he's saying not matching the address Jim gave me because I recognized it enough to know it's local, and my voice rises in alarm. "You're taking me out of the city?"

"No, Simone, calm down." He grabs my hand again, holding onto it more firmly this time, his response in the clipped tone I've already come to hate. "I own a place here in the city, although it is not under my name because I value my privacy."

My indignation deflates as fast as it arrived. "Oh."

His voice softens and something tells me he's grinning even though I can't see him. "I am pleased you attempted to research me; however, it gave you a glimpse into a life I am no longer actively engaged in."

"I don't take anyone's word anymore. Looking you up seemed like a good idea considering I don't know anything about you and you're not exactly forthcoming."

"I promise you it will not stay that way." A pause, then, "I hope you like the dress."

"I do. Thank you, although I could've worn something of my own—"

"No," he cuts in while sliding closer to me, invading my personal space and setting my senses on alert, releasing his hold on my hand. "Your outfit the other night made it clear the rest of your wardrobe no doubt leaves something to be desired. It was, and will remain, my pleasure to give you something nice."

"Isaac—"

The warm feel of his now free hand sliding along my jaw before cupping my cheek makes me suck in a breath of surprise, chasing away the words while my whole focus shifts to his touch, and the insane way my body responds as if it knows him.

He brings his face so close to mine I can feel his breath against my mouth when he speaks. "I love the sound of my name on those lovely lips of yours. Say it again and I am sure my hands will misbehave."

"Aren't they already?"

He drops his hands and sits back so quick the unexpected action leaves me feeling bereft and strangely alone. I wonder if I said the wrong thing and am about to ask him when the car stops moving and shuts off, which can only mean we've reached our destination.

He raps once on the window with his knuckles and moves close to me again but without us touching, and declares, "I have made a decision."

"About what?" It's an unconscious decision, when it comes out as a whisper, but I see Jim's shadow out the window and for some reason am paranoid he can hear us.

"You."

"Oh," I whisper. "What about me?"

He grabs my chin between his fingers and I feel his breath mingling with mine as he says near my mouth, "You have two choices: you can tell me to take you home and I will leave you alone forever, or you can say my name and I will feed you as I promised."

"So no dinner if I don't want things to go farther? That's hardly fair."

His low chuckle sends a chill through me, his proximity making it so I feel it as well. His thumb gives a light stroke to my chin as his laughter dies away. "I never proclaimed myself as fair."

"Well, in that case, I choose a new third option: you feed me like you promised, show me your lair, and let me decide if you're the kind of animal I wanna take on."

"Animal?"

Amusement definitely laces his question, and I nod, knowing he can feel it before I clarify with a shaky breath. "It's as if you're two steps ahead of me right now. You have to let me catch up before you pounce like a wild cat with a piece of meat trapped in his paws."

"You have got quite the sassy mouth on you." Moving away, he opens the door and light streams in as he extends an arm, indicating I should get out. "Shall we?"

"Oh, I win?"

"One time bonus. It is your lucky night."

Something tells me the fact I didn't say to take me home makes him the lucky one and he's well aware of it. Holding my hand as I get out of the car, he follows closely behind me, and once we're both standing on the sidewalk Jim shuts the door.

"Anything else, sir?"

"No, thank you. I will take it from here, Jim."

"Of course."

Jim walks one way, we walk the other, and not even a minute later we're inside the building, going up on the elevator. He's released my hand, now leaning against the wall opposite me with his arms crossed as he stares at me, which reminds me of the other night at the restaurant when he waited for me outside.

"I was correct. You are stunning in that dress."

God, I love his voice, with its deep, smooth tone, and his barely-there English inflection. It makes me wish he would keep talking until I get sick of hearing him, but I don't think that will ever happen. His voice is perfect and I'm already a sucker for it.

Flicking my gaze away, I lift my eyes to stare at the digital screen as it counts the floors, my fingers fiddling with my purse as he continues to focus on me as if I were his prey, just as I accused him of being the predator in the car.

In an attempt to divert the conversation, I smirk and flash him a glance. "Why do you live in an apartment if you wish for privacy? Don't people recognize you here?"

"I rarely leave while I am here, but this is a private elevator which only leads to one place. The top floor penthouse. Mine."

The last word comes out with a growl and some part of me think he's not talking just about his place; that he's talking about me too. And I'm excited even though perhaps I shouldn't be, but we both know I'm not going to walk away, even if I pretend I'm thinking about what to do.

Not much I can say to that so instead I give him a bright smile as the elevator comes to a stop. "So, what's for dinner?"

6

SIMONE

THE ANSWER to my question is answered almost immediately when we enter, as dinner is set out on a table for two near closed balcony doors, in a room with muted lighting. The view through the glass, however, is amazing and after Isaac removes my coat, I walk over to the doors and stare out them. There's a clear view of the lake behind the building and the almost full moon shines bright, reflecting off the water.

"It's beautiful."

"I know. The view is why I chose this apartment over all the other ones shown to me." The fact he's right behind me when he says this, and I didn't hear him walk up, makes me jump. He chuckles and puts his hands on my shoulders. "Let's eat, hmm?"

He walks away when I nod, pulling out my chair with a smile. He takes his seat once I've taken mine, and I give a small gasp of surprise when Jim steps out of the shadows without a word, lifting the covers away from our dinner plates.

Laughter escapes me when I see what's for dinner: spaghetti and meatballs.

"How did you know this is my fave?"

The lift of Isaac's right eyebrow is simultaneous with his sudden smirk. Raising his fork, he twirls some of the pasta around his spoon while nodding at my plate, once again ignoring my inquiry. "Eat while it is hot."

I do as we fall into a companionable silence, and when I've eaten half of my plate, I glance over at Isaac to find him frowning at me. Dropping the fork, I lower my eyes, pulling the napkin off my lap to wipe at the corners of my mouth before deciding to speak.

"What?" He says nothing so I bring my eyes back to his and mimic his glower. "Why do you look mad?"

His face instantly softens as he places his fork down on his plate and picks up his glass to sip his drink. "Apologies. I am not mad; well, not with you, at least. It is clear from watching you eat that you are not well fed. You were eating as if it is the last good meal you will have, and I am angry. Rightly so, if you ask me."

A sad, but accurate observation. I don't eat properly. I spend most of my money on taking care of my son and while I do get some assistance, it's not enough for much of anything. Most days I eat once a day, rarely do I eat twice. I don't know what to say or do, so picking up my fork once again, I nod at Isaac before dropping my gaze back to my plate to focus on eating.

He doesn't let me finish though. I've about a third left when he speaks.

"Stop, Simone." As I drop the fork with a sniffle, he reaches across the table and snatches my hand, saying nothing until I look up at him with teary eyes. "You must not stuff yourself after eating so little for a while as it will make you sick. Jim will pack the leftovers and extras for you to take home. I would not wish them wasted."

"But, you—"

He releases my hand and stands up, his abrupt movement cutting off my reply, and then holds his hand out again for me to take. "I have plenty of food and, as your luck would have it, a particular distaste for leftovers, so they are yours to receive. Now, come with me."

Taking his hand once I've risen, he tugs me close to his side and says to Jim, "Thank you. I'll let you know when it is time to take Miss Winston home."

Isaac leads the way to another room, which surprisingly isn't the living room, but a small library. After having me take a seat in a dark blue winged-back chair, he sits in the one to my immediate left, and with the press of a button, a flame bursts to life in the fireplace in front of us.

"What are your thoughts on my lair thus far, Simone?"

My cheeks flame at his reminder of my words earlier, and after flicking my gaze around the quite lovely and cozy room, I smile softly at him. "It's very welcoming. Masculine and warm without being sterile and nearly colorless."

"I spend a lot of time at home. I would not wish to live in a cold environment, nor would you, I presume."

He wouldn't like my apartment then. Not that it is barren or anything, but it's certainly leagues below this one in attractiveness. It's meant for utility, not for pleasing the eye, especially at its low price tag. And all my furniture is stuff I either found or was given, things people were going to throw away, and none in good shape for sure.

Certainly nothing as divine as this chair I'm sitting in, but the urge to get up and walk around is undeniable.

"No, I can't say I would." Standing up, I feel him watching as I walk over to one of the bookshelves, but he doesn't follow me with anything other than his intense gaze. "Have you read all the books in here?"

"Yes. Only my favorites deserve space on a shelf. All the others are given away to those who might appreciate them in a way I do not."

"I see."

"I am sure you do."

Running my index finger over the spines, I tilt my head to the side as I read the titles on them, and other than the sounds of the fire crackling, both he and I remain quiet. I can't help but wonder what he's thinking, what he sees in me, or why I'm even here. He doesn't seem in a rush to get to the point, and I'm not sure if that's a good or bad thing. Either way, it's been clear from the moment he walked me home that his eye is on me, and has been, and I've no doubt I'll find out the answers to any questions I have or will have sooner rather than later.

"How long have you worked at the restaurant, Simone?"

Keeping my eyes on the books, my answer is simple. "A little under a year."

"And what did you do before then?"

"Nothing. This is my first job."

"I see."

"I'm sure you do."

He laughs at hearing his own reply tossed back at him, making me smile until he asks, "If you did not work before this job, what did you do to survive?"

I'm sure he knows the answer; he just wants me to give him the information instead, so I oblige even as my smile dies as quick as it arrived. "I was married and stayed home at his request. We're divorced now."

"You are a little young to already be divorced."

"Perhaps the truth is I married too young."

"Touché."

I expect him to ask me why I got divorced, but he doesn't, so I ask, "Ever been married?"

"No."

Which I knew already, of course, but stating or asking things we already know seems to be the game he wants to play. "Well, it's definitely not all everyone makes it out to be. So perhaps you should celebrate having dodged such a bullet."

"Do you not desire to marry again, Simone?"

Turning to face him, he still sits in the chair, his intense and commanding gaze focused on me as his fingers lazily tap the cloth-covered arms of the chair. As if he's thinking, plotting; what exactly I don't know because his eyes are also guarded.

With a bright smile, I clasp both my hands in front of me, and throw the question back at him without answering, deliberately refusing to give into calling him by name. "Do you wish to ever marry at all?"

"I do."

"Why?" When he simply raises a brow, I clarify. "For one who requires such privacy, surely a marriage would jeopardize your solitude? Your life lived under the prized cloak of night?"

At that, he chuckles, shaking his head as he holds out a hand palm up, and commands, "Come here."

Taking a few steps forward, nothing prepares me for the jolt of electricity as our hands meet, nor for him to tighten his grasp and yank me until I land in his lap. My heart thumps; not in terror, but inexplicable excitement, as I realize I must've poked the animal too hard in his cage. I knew I ran that chance; he doesn't seem like the type of man who allows anything he does or wants in his life to be questioned.

"If you want to go home, Simone," he says in a low, desire filled voice as he perches me on his lap at what one would consider a reasonable, gentlemanly distance. "Well, now is your chance."

"And if I don't? What happens if I choose to stay?"

Lifting a hand, he takes one finger and places it in the crook of my neck, then slowly drags it down along the curve before straightening it and heading down the center of my chest. The dress I'm wearing has a v-neck bodice, one that dips enough the side of my breasts are visible, and he pauses his descent between them.

With hooded eyes, and a voice which seems to thicken by the second, he says, "If you consent to stay, then we will discuss what your future with me will entail, and what I desire from you. I will also give you a taste of what is to come, since your eyes and body are near to begging for it. That is, if you wish it."

The old me would've gone running at a statement filled with such blatant intent, having been filled with such fear at the mere idea that I failed to see the possibilities, not that I particularly saw them now. I'm not sure what a man like him…would want with a woman like me. It's an unmistakable fact we are from two different worlds, but I decide if he's going to ignore it, than so am I. However, not blindly; never, ever again would I trust someone mindlessly.

"What do you want from me? I think it's only fair you tell me before I say yes or no." When he doesn't answer, his face not even moving a muscle, I realize he isn't going to answer me. Nevertheless, I keep trying anyway. "That's the second time you've given me the option to walk away. Is it your secret hope that I do?"

That's all it takes. The animal I called him earlier comes unleashed, evident in the coiling of his body as it tightens in preparation of pouncing, and the way his hands slide to my upper arms, clasping them in an unyielding grip. His eyes narrow as he draws me closer, leaning toward me with equal measure, until our faces are so close we would be kissing if either of us pursed our lips.

After a moments pause, where we stare at

each other, and I don't even so much as quiver in his hold, he asks, "What are you feeling as I hold you like this? Do you fear me? The unknown, perhaps?"

"If I feared you," I answer honestly, instinctively knowing it is what he requires. "I wouldn't be here. If I feared anything at all in regard to you, I wouldn't be here."

"And?"

"Nothing," I whisper, replying to the rest of his question. "I feel nothing."

His face goes from neutral to amused, a wolfish grin stealing over his lips, the corner of his eyes creasing with genuine mirth as he lets out a deep chuckle. "This is the one and only time I will let you get away with lying to me, Simone. I bet if I slid my hand between your legs this instant, your lust would be undeniable. I would say that is feeling something, wouldn't you?"

I whimper as his fingers dig into my skin, his eyes glinting as they sear into mine, both our bodies radiating with heat as he continues without giving me a chance to answer.

"Being approached by a man in the dark, your natural instinct should be to run from him in fear. Your gaze, your body, they shouldn't hunger for him. You should want to protect yourself, to make sure he means well before you are in his home, sitting in his lap, held in his grip with no escape. But not you, Simone."

I close my eyes as his words fill me with a shame I haven't felt since I was first kidnapped, as if I had asked for it, or done something to deserve it. A shame, which had quickly dissipated when I realized I enjoyed every second of what happened, when I realized something was wrong with me, and I didn't care. The same way I hadn't cared until this very moment, having walked into this man's house and his arms without fear, without worry.

"Do not hide from me," he commands, his softening tone accompanied by a barely there kiss against my lips to get my attention. "Open your eyes and do not close them again. You have no reason to."

Even the graze of his lips confuses me after his previous statement, and when my eyes are once more focused on his, he tilts his head a little to the side as if to study me. Continuing to grip one arm, he releases the other and lowers his hand out of sight. Feeling him slide the palm of his hand up my bare leg to my thigh and under the slit in the skirt, wondering what he plans to do makes me shiver, but he simply chuckles once more and adjusts our positions until I'm straddling his lap.

Using both hands, he grabs my hips and yanks me toward him, until my dress is barely covering my ass, my legs are bare, and I'm able to feel how turned on he is. Pelvis to pelvis, I start imagining all the things he could do to me right now, which makes me let out a moan as my hips move a little involuntarily.

I can't help it; I don't want to. I've been attracted to him since the moment I laid eyes on him, and something in him calls to me. It's the only reason I'm here, desiring to know everything about him. Desiring to get as close as possible.

He's right, I do feel something. But it's nothing negative. I feel curious, lusty, and being in his arms, sexy, because it's obvious he wants me in a sexual way.

I haven't felt sexy in so long, not since…

Not since before I found out about my pregnancy.

I love my son, but having him changed my body. Height-wise, I'm five-five, and before pregnancy, I was a mere one hundred and ten pounds. But my boobs got bigger, I put on a good bit of weight as I hit one-fifty by forty weeks, and now I have curves I didn't before. My weight hovers around one-thirty. It wasn't a huge change, but enough for me to have to learn to love my new body, and while I know he's only been born four months, I'm fairly sure this is the weight I'll sustain. It's not really a bad thing; I always knew I was a bit underweight for my height.

I just haven't been sure anyone would consider me attractive, but now I know there is no question.

Isaac definitely wants me. And I want him.

Ready to let him know it, I don't even get the chance as he speaks, his words soft with an underlying current of desire.

"Let your hair down." He keeps his grip on my hips, although they flex as if he wishes to move them, to touch or assist me in following his wishes. "I wish to see you without it up."

Nervous but willing to see where this could go, I nod and lift my arms, feeling the soft material of the dress flutter against me, especially on my breasts. This dress doesn't allow for a bra, the movement making my nipples go taut with arousal, and I carefully remove the pins holding my bun in place.

His deep hum of approval in his throat is something I feel down to where our bodies are practically connected were it not for the material in the way as my hair drops around my shoulders. It's a slightly darker brown than his, and a bit wavy naturally. I try to even it out and make sure there are no tangles, running my hands through it while arranging it around my shoulders evenly, while one of his hands moves behind my back. There, his hand teases the end of my hair, which almost reaches the top of my ass.

"Gorgeous," he murmurs as he releases my hips, slipping both hands under my hair, and after a moment gathers it together. I'm not sure if he's got it in one hand only until the other comes up to cup my face, the thumb gently stroking my cheek. "You are so fucking gorgeous."

At those words, I pause, my breath catching in my throat at hearing the familiar phrase. Master had been the only one to ever tell me I was 'so fucking gorgeous' and I stare at Isaac, confused because it's just not right.

He isn't him.

And crazy as it is, I'm in love with Master, so what am I doing on this man's lap?

You're never going to see him again, my brain screams at me. *You don't even know who the hell he is. What makes you think he'll come after you?*

Isaac must see something in my face in reaction to what he's said, and I don't know what, but he frowns and lets go of my hair and hip as if I've burned him. I scramble off his lap almost in reflex to him letting go, the pins still held between my fingers, and frantically try to put up my hair as I try to put distance between us.

As if it matters.

"You wish to return home."

It's a statement, not a question, and I give him a curt nod even though I'm still so lost. He stares at me for a few more seconds, looking as if he wishes to say something, yet seems to decide against it as he turns on his heel and exits the room.

After what feels like an eternity, he returns with my coat and purse, Jim standing in the corner of the entryway with a neutral expression on his face. I wonder for an instant where he stayed here in the apartment while we were alone.

Once I'm in my coat, Isaac leans in and kisses me chastely on the cheek, saying, "Jim will see you home."

"What?" He draws his face away, his face cold now, and takes a step back. "You're not coming?"

"I do not think it would be wise for us to be alone any longer. Thank you for dining with me. I bid you a good evening."

"Isaac—"

His gaze burns bright at my use of his name, but with a firming of his lips and a shake of his head, he leaves me alone with Jim. My lips tremble, confusion and humiliation and thwarted lust whirling around in my stomach as Jim steps up next to me, placing a gentle hand on my elbow to guide me out of the apartment.

It's quiet all the way from his place to mine, and as we reach my door, Jim stops at the top of the steps while I pull out my keys. I probably shouldn't ask him anything, say anything, yet I can't resist because I don't understand.

"What did I do wrong?"

He frowns, looking at me helplessly. "I don't know, Miss Winston. I wasn't in the room. He simply said you wished to return home."

"Oh." With my hand on the doorknob, I give him a sad smile. "Is that it then?"

"Sorry, I can't speak for him. I only do what he tells me to. However…" He reaches into his jacket pocket and pulls out a white card, handing it to me with a smile. "If you ever need anything, anything at all, that's my personal number. I wish you well, Miss Winston."

I feel like crying as he walks away, putting my key into the lock and stepping inside as quiet as I can. The lights are off, which means my son is sleeping and so is Helen. When I go to slip the card he handed me into my purse, it feels as if something is in there, so I quietly head to the kitchen and turn on a light.

Then, I pull out the envelope shoved inside, opening it to discover a pile of bills.

Twenty crisp one-hundred dollar bills, to be exact.

And I sit down at my rickety little table and weep into my hands.

"I AM NOT sure what I did to spook you."

It's been a whole month since I heard his voice, so when it comes out of nowhere as I walk out of work, I can't help but jump.

"Isaac!" I cover the exaggerated beating of my heart with my hand and scowl at him even though it's dark as he walks toward me. "Seriously, what the fuck?"

"Pardon?" He stops under the streetlight, his beautiful face illuminated for a second before he steps out of it, and into my path. "I believe that is the first time I have heard you swear."

"Really? In all the time we've spent together? Imagine that." He doesn't respond to my clear sarcasm — because we haven't known each other that long which would explain his lack of knowledge about my 'potty mouth' — and I cross my arms over my chest, continuing to frown at him. "Why are you here?"

"I wish to apologize for whatever I did to make you look at me as if you did not know why you were sitting in my lap that night."

"Oh." I'm not sure how to answer that, because how do I tell him I'm in love with someone I've never fucking seen, nor do I know their name? Yeah, he'll think I'm a psycho, if he doesn't already. So I try and divert his attention with something that's bugged me since we met. "Why do you talk like that?"

"Sorry, talk like what?"

"Ever heard of contractions? You talk like you've got a stick up your ass."

Even in the shadows, I can see his mouth turn down as he furrows his brows as if he doesn't understand. "The way I speak bothers you? Why?"

"It's weird."

"Ah, I see. Is it not obvious I am weird in every conceivable capacity?"

Huffing, I drop my arms to my sides, resisting the urge to touch him by fisting my hands. "Quite obvious. And if you don't mind, I need to get home now."

"Shall I walk you?"

"No." He doesn't move out of my way and when I try to step around him, he lets me, but then falls into step beside me. This causes me to snap, "I said no. Are you deaf?"

"Silly question. You speak, I hear you and respond, so it is clear I am not deaf."

I refuse to smile at his antics, or the humor in his voice, or the way he's joking with me. "What do you want, Isaac?"

"For you to say my name with less irritation while I am fucking you in my bed."

Maybe I should've expected it, but I didn't, and his matter of fact statement causes me to lose my concentration. I trip over something — who fucking knows what — and within a breath I'm wrapped in his arms. Speaking of breath, being in his arms steals mine, especially as the way he's holding me positions me close to his face, and I smell the cinnamon on his. I wonder if it's his toothpaste, or if he ate something cinnamon, and if he will taste as good as he smells.

Then I realize I don't want to feel that way and take it out on him.

Raising a brow at him, I ask with a sneer, "What's the going rate for actually getting me to fuck you instead of just letting you grope me on your lap? Four thousand?"

"Is that how much you want?"

He probably did it to get a reaction out of me, I realize too late, but that's what he gets. I lift a hand and haul off, slapping him across the face, expecting him to let me go almost immediately.

My slap is hard enough his head jerks a little to the side, but instead of getting angry, he lets out a deep, dark sounding chuckle. And suddenly I know he got exactly what he wished out of me, because if he wasn't aroused before, he is now. I feel his cock pressing against me, demanding attention as his hold tightens on me.

Honesty in this moment demands I admit how turned on I am too. My attraction for him hasn't gone away; if anything it's gotten stronger. I barely know him, but I've missed him. He makes me feel a way I haven't felt in a while, and part of me hates him for it. Especially since he makes me realize what I'm missing by being alone.

Instead of commenting on the slap though, or my extremely rude and inaccurate comment about the money, he lifts his hand to my face and gently caresses my cheek. "Tell me what I did to make you feel this way."

"Nothing." His face darkens at the blatant lie, and I remember what he said about lying, but fuck, he doesn't own me. I don't have to explain myself, and I glare right back at him. "Let me go."

He ignores my request, asking, "Is there someone in your life, Simone? Have I overstepped?"

Is it possible for him to overstep in my situation? I don't think so, but... "No. It has nothing to do with you." Since he continues holding me, and just gazing at me as if confounded, my next question comes out in a clear, aggravated way. "Don't you have anyone else to stalk?"

"No. Just you."

His answer should alarm me, I know it should, but it doesn't.

God, I'm fucked up.

"I don't understand," I blurt out, finally breaking and asking him what I've wanted to since the first time I saw him in the diner. "Why me? I'm nothing special!"

"Ah, but you are." He turns around and in front of us by the curb is the car with Jim holding the door open. Isaac doesn't even give me a chance to say anything or protest; he simply carries me over and puts me inside, then follows while rubbing his hands together as he sits on the seat across from me. "Much warmer. Now, where were we?"

Jim shuts the door and moments later the car starts to move as I glare at Isaac. "You can't just come take me off the fucking street."

"Three times in one evening. Shall we go for four?"

"I can swear if I want to," I say while crossing my arms over my chest and staring at the window. "I'm an adult and you don't own me."

A beat of silence, followed by a soft reply. "I would like to."

Whipping my face back to his, my eyes widen as my mouth drops open, which I quickly snap shut to retort, "You've got to be fucking kidding me right now."

"Four."

"Stop counting!"

"I am keeping track for later."

I feel like throwing a fit, but somehow refrain even though I'm pretty sure if my eyes could spit fire, they would at him right now. "Keeping track for what? They are just descriptive words, fit for when one is angry, or—or—"

"In the bedroom?"

My cheeks flame as the corners of his mouth lift in a smirk. "Screw you."

"That can be done anywhere." My face burns hotter as he reaches across the space between us and pulls me to him, catching me as I tumble onto his lap, arranging me to straddle him before trapping me in his arms, my arms caught tight between our bodies. "Like right here." He lowers his voice as he brings his mouth close to my ear, placing a kiss just underneath the lobe to make me shiver, and whispering, "Technically, I am counting the amount of your punishment. It is five; one for lying, four for swearing."

He doesn't seem fazed by the fact I stiffen in his arms at the mention of being punished like a damned child, one hand tightening around me to keep me still as the other slowly glides up my back and into the hair at the nape of my neck, spreading wide before gripping it, and pulling my head back with a firm tug.

I cry out as he bares my neck, my eyes slamming shut as the feeling throwing me back to the last time this was done hits me square in the heart, and I can't decide if the cry is one of pleasure or pain. He runs his mouth down the side of my neck first, and then he starts going to the center, but instead of his lips, he drags his teeth across the surface. His grip on my hair increases and I whimper at the way my body bows back a little more, followed seconds later by him finding a spot bared right above my breast and sucking hard enough I know it'll leave a mark.

He keeps me in this position as if it's effortless, for what feels like the ride of my life, kissing and marking up the area above my breasts while breathing easy the whole time. My neck starts to ache, but I don't say no, I don't tell him to stop, because deep down I don't want him to. I like the fact he's taking charge, he's just doing what we both want, yet something I would turn down if he asked permission. I give him consent with my silence, and we both know it, even though I'm not sure how the lines became so clear with zero discussion.

With my back bowed, there's no chance to escape as he frees his other arm, which he slips under my shirt from the front, and cups a breast in his hand.

At the same time he gives it a squeeze, his lips lift my chest and he asks, "Do you wish to stay in the life you have, Simone?"

"No." My heart beats faster, since I know exactly what he wishes from me by his 'owning me' comment earlier, and say, "But at least it's mine."

Removing his hand from beneath my shirt, he says nothing for a moment, making me wonder what will happen next, but that's answered in the hand landing above my breasts. It slides up until my neck is cradled in the curve between his thumb and forefinger, yet he doesn't tighten it. He just leaves it there; promising or threatening, I can't say. Either way, I'm not afraid.

"I did not intend to insult you with the money. I merely wished to pay you for your time, and make things easier for you." His thumb strokes my neck in a slow, hypnotic manner. "I hope you used it to make your life less painful."

Right now, right here in this moment, he makes me feel desirable, cared about, confused, and nervous, all in one. Even as I'm in a position where he could hurt me if he desires, I get the feeling he won't; not unless I want him to. And I don't know how I know that; I don't know him. He doesn't know me.

But I feel as if we've been here before even though I've gone over it time and again in my head. Master spoke differently, he smelled differently, and he certainly hadn't been gentle. Could Isaac tell though? Does he sense where I've been, what I went through, and is that why he's targeted me?

More than that, is it bad I'm not afraid of him at all, and wonder what 'owning' me would entail in his eyes? And the even bigger question is, with how much he obviously knows about me, does he truly know what taking care of me would mean, such as the fact I have a child without a father?

"What do you want from me, Isaac? I thought you were gone a month ago, and now you're back. Stop messing with me."

"I was going to let you go. I tried to stay away, but earlier this evening, I realized that is not going to happen. You are meant for me, and I will make you mine."

I force my eyes to open at his words, and that's when I realize we've been driving for longer than it takes to get to my place, or even to his apartment. There is no light posts to shine in the car, I can't see his face, and that means he's taking me out of town.

"Isaac, what the fuck do you think you're doing." I don't even struggle because I know it's pointless, but I'm practically whispering as my eyes fill with tears. "Take me home, right now. You can't do this!"

It's dumb to say it because he has done it. With almost a painful rip through my body, panic and fear return from their long vacation with a vengeance when he doesn't say anything, and I don't know what I do, but in the next few seconds pain shoots through me as I land on the floor of the car between the seats. I gasp for air at the same time I start sobbing, and he curses above me. I hear the window between us and Jim speak.

"Yes, sir?"

"How long until we arrive?"

"Ten minutes."

"Call ahead and have the doctor waiting, please. Simone has hurt herself and I want him waiting as I am not sure I should move her. And hurry, if you can."

"Absolutely, sir."

I hear the window close and sob louder, hating both of them right then. Unable to understand how Jim could let him take me away like this, even help him, even though I know he works for him. He doesn't have any loyalty to me, but god, I thought he was kind. I thought they both were.

No wonder I married an idiot; I am one as well.

I moan, trying to move in hope of lessening the pain, and Isaac's hand comes down to hold me still.

"God, do not fucking move. I swear I heard something crack when you landed. I let you go when you started to freak out because I did not wish to hurt you, not realizing you would not expect it and fail to protect yourself."

The discomfort I'm feeling brings truth to his words, and I wonder if that's why I feel like I can't breathe. I think the car speeds up, but I'm not sure, and right as I lose consciousness, the last thing I hear is Isaac bellow Jim's name.

8

SIMONE

WHEN I REAWAKEN, nothing makes sense immediately.

I'm in a soft bed so it's obvious I'm not at home, my chest aches so I know the part in the car happened, but I hear my son giggling. Trying to see where he could be in the room or if I'm hearing things, I try to move, only to moan as a sharp pain ripples through my chest, my eyes slamming shut again from the sheer force of it.

"Malik," I manage to whisper through the raw pain in my throat. "Where…?"

"Shh, relax." It's Helen speaking, and her touch on my arm instantly comforts me, easing my growing alarm. "You don't want to be sedated again, do you?"

For many reasons, I don't, but for many others — like the fire in my chest — I think I do. But all I wanna know about is my baby, so I repeat, "Malik?"

"He's fine sweetie. Charming the staff, got them wrapped around his little fingers. He's playing on the floor across the room right now."

Ah, so we are at Isaac's, but... "How?"

"We were waiting for you here. I swear when he pulled up and I saw you on the floor of the car, he put his hands up like he knew I was gonna hurt him if he hurt you. He said, 'she flipped out' and I said, 'I told you so.' But he said you didn't give him a chance to explain."

My head hurts along with my chest, and I breathe through the pain as the words come out stunted. "I thought...he was...kidnapping me."

"Well, that's just absurd, dear. He's a very recognizable man, who has been seen with you in the restaurant, and I have all his information that you gave me. Why would you think for a moment he'd do such a foolish thing?"

"I..." What could I possibly say? That it happened before? There's no way she would understand. "What didn't he get to explain then? Why are we here?"

She sighs, and when she speaks, I can hear the smile in her voice. "He came to the apartment last night looking for you. He asked where you were and I told him you took an extra shift, that I babysit for you. I only knew it was him 'cause he had his little undertaker with him. I let them in and I swear, you should've seen both their faces.

They were horrified at seeing the little hovels we live in."

"I bet. I read about this place. Is it as big as it sounds?"

"Huge. But very light on staff. Seems he likes his privacy."

I frown. "And you sound like you like him."

"You've been in and out for three days. We've spent a bit of time together." When I gasp, she laughs and squeezes my hand with hers. "You needed to stay still, but kept freaking out, which is why I said for you to relax so they wouldn't need to sedate you again. You seem better now though."

I don't remember waking up at all. The last thing I do recall is lying on the floor of the car, and him holding me down, before passing out. I must've freaked out more than I thought.

"Anyway, he insisted all he wants to do is take care of you. He seemed really agitated and kind of angry that you lived like that, but I dunno why. It's not like tons of people don't live like that. He didn't even blink when I insisted I come with you here."

"Did he…" I lick my lips but my mouth is so dry it doesn't do anything, so I ask, "Water?"

"Oh, yeah." I feel something touch my lips a second later, and realizing it's a straw, take a few drinks before she takes it away.

Wetting my lips now, I go back to what I wanna know. "Did he know about my son?"

"Yes."

She pauses, as if she wants to say something but is thinking better of it, so I try to encourage her. "Is there something you wanna say?"

"Are you sure there's nothing you wanna tell me sweetie?"

There's only one thing I haven't told her and there's no way she would've guessed. "Uh, not sure what you mean."

"You sure you've never met him before the time at your work?"

Laughing, I tug my hand from hers and drag my eyes open to look at her, only to see she's staring across the room. "Positive. Do you honestly think I'd forget someone like him?"

"No." She sighs, and tosses a smile my way, before looking away again. "He just comes across like he knows you. Maybe that's just the kind of person he is. Malik likes him, so that's something at least. Should never trust anyone a baby doesn't like."

I'm not sure what to say to that. Seems like he won over my family — I consider Helen family because she's like the mom I never had — while I slept. I'm glad it wasn't what I thought, although now I'll have to apologize for reacting that way.

Opening my mouth, I'm just about to ask her

78

where he is when I hear him ask, "Has she awakened?"

Helen nods, giving me a final quick smile, and says, "I'll just take Malik downstairs for a snack while you two talk."

He hasn't moved into my line of vision, and after she's left the room and shut the door behind her, the continued silence from him makes me nervous enough to break it.

"Isaac?"

"This is not how I wished to bring you into my home."

"Didn't think asking me when you approached me after work was a better idea?" I can't see him and I refuse to lift my head; I'm just too tired. "She told me you came to my place. It's obvious you thought I would be home. What if I had told you no?"

"I still would have brought you here, but I should have realized you would worry about your son and eased your fears. However," he says, finally stepping up to the side of the bed into my line of vision with a frown on his face. "I believe you had no intentions of telling me about him. You assumed I did not know you had him?"

Staring at him, I don't think I need to explain, but I say anyway, "I'm his mother. It's my job to protect him."

"I understand," he says gently. "But births are public records."

And he made it clear he knew all about me by his actions alone; I should've known. At another twinge of pain in my chest, I ask, "Want to tell me why the hell my chest hurts so badly I can't move?"

"You cracked a rib and bruised a few others when you fell. It should heal in a month or so, but you will have to take it easy."

"Meaning you want me to lay here and let you take care of me."

He leans in, clasping my hand in his, and brings his mouth close to mine. "Why do I get the impression you are offended by my desire to take care of you?"

"Because none of this makes sense. It hasn't since we met." I shut my eyes because his gaze is so intensely focused on mine, his lips not even an inch away, and his smell surrounds me. I don't want him to affect me like he does. "I don't need you to rescue me."

"I disagree."

"You can't keep me here if I don't want you to."

"Again, I disagree. I can do many things. Now, whether or not I do them, that is different." He pauses when I huff, but when I don't say anything further, he asks, "What happened with your husband, Simone? Why did you leave him?"

Isaac seems like he's the kind of guy who

would beat up someone who did what my husband did to me, so I go with the less bad decision he made. "He cheated on me."

"Did he? Asshole."

I can't help but let a smile slip through at his choice of words, but it's quickly followed by a downturn of my mouth as I recount what happened. "Yes, he did. I walked in on her sucking his dick after…well, after I'd been gone for a while."

"I see." A lull in conversation, then, "Does he know about the boy?"

"No." I figure what he's getting at — is he the father — and answer accordingly. "He isn't my son's father. And no, I don't wish to talk about it."

Even as I say the last part, I feel myself starting to drift off, and I'm not positive, yet I think he makes a sound in the back of his throat. Then, after gently clearing his throat, he asks in a soft tone, "I will let you rest, but will you answer me one thing first?"

"Hmm?"

"Why did you name him Malik?"

Random, but the question brings an affectionate smile to my face, because of the meaning behind it. To Isaac I simply say, "Because it reminds me of his father and he's all I have of him."

His hand tightens on mine, his lips brush

against mine in a whisper of a kiss, followed up by a softly spoken, "Rest now."

Then, he's gone as quietly as he arrived, and the sound of the door shutting is the last thing I remember before falling asleep.

9

ISAAC

WHEN EVERYBODY GOES to bed for the evening, Isaac heads to his office, and Jim joins him not long after.

"She does not know." Isaac sits with his head in his hands, his words muffled. "How is this possible?"

"Are you sure, sir?"

"Yes. Fucking one-hundred-percent. If I could beat that fucker again, I would."

"You didn't know, sir. You followed the same protocol for everyone. The signatures were done by two different people on the consent form. Someone checks that for you for this very reason. You had no way to know it wasn't she who signed it." He sighs, clearly aware of the way his employer has felt for a while now. "You placed your trust in other people's honesty and it worked for three years. You didn't do anything wrong."

"I did. I should have guessed. She did not fight. Even those who are playing fought to make it more real. She did not and she thought—" He chokes on his words, pausing to take a deep breath and clear his throat before continuing. "Why? God, she gave in. And…fuck, I want to rip his goddamned throat out. He turned me into a fucking criminal."

"You're not. And she doesn't seem angry to me, sir. She could've reported it. She didn't."

Isaac doesn't have a response to that, at least, not out loud. Because really, what could she have possibly said? There is no way that dumb-fuck of a husband she had would admit what he had done to the cops, because he committed a crime. And she knew nothing of where she had been or who had taken her, and nobody had reported her missing because apparently, her husband had been the only person she knew. He couldn't even imagine how she felt to realize what that asshole had done to her.

And then, Isaac had walked in and saw Simone there in the restaurant. A lot of miles away from where he had dropped her off that final morning, looking ill-fed, poorly dressed, and exhausted. She hadn't seen him that time because he didn't understand why she would be there appearing that way and had turned right out the door of the restaurant and left. He waited around, followed her home, and when he saw her husband nowhere in sight, he started investigating.

And then he had located the bastard, found out what happened, and beat the fucking shit out of him. He's still breathing though. Isaac is a lot of things, but a murderer — or a rapist, for fucks sake — he isn't. And there was no way the moron would go to the cops, because they both knew he deserved the ass kicking Isaac gave him.

He lives far away from his clients for a reason. He never wants to run into them. He knows what they look like, but they don't because it's a fantasy. Something they pay for; it isn't meant to be real, just *feel* real. They are given instructions, safe-words, and contracts to sign so he never does anything they don't want, and if they say the word, they go home immediately. Game over.

So, how the hell had he gotten it so wrong when she'd been under his care?

To see her like that at her work, to find out what had truly gone on, he had been sick for weeks when he realized what he'd been inadvertently involved in. He came close to turning himself in one time, but instead, he decided to make it up to her.

Problem is, he doesn't know how to do that.

And it's especially important he figures it out now that he's sure the child is his.

Not that he's really questioned it since he had lain eyes on him for the first time just the other day. Little Malik is the spitting image of him when he was a child, and he has the pictures to prove it. And now there is no way he wants to let them go if he can help it.

He isn't sure how he will tell her, or how she will react, but he doesn't want her to run when he does. He just couldn't stand to know she lived like that for a second longer, not when she is the mother of his child. Taking care of her and Malik is now his duty, and one he won't fail.

"Do you think she told Helen?"

Jim's question causes him to jump out of his thoughts, and he shakes his head. "No. It appears she kept it to herself completely."

"She might turn into a problem, don't you think?"

Amusement filters into Isaac's voice as he speaks, lifting a brow in question at the only person he trusts with his life. "I cannot say, but it is clear you two do not like each other. Why is that?"

"She's getting suspicious," Jim continues, ignoring the question. "You haven't known the girl long in her knowledge. To want to bring her to live with you is odd, and you know it."

"What else could I have done? There is no way I would continue letting my child and her live in such a situation. She found my giving her that money insulting. I could hardly offer to put her in a better place; no doubt she would have been insulted with that as well."

"She told me earlier she asked the girl if you've met before, as if she had figured something out, and she insisted you haven't."

Isaac scoffs, shoving a hand through his hair. "Well, anyone who looks at the child and me close might suspect we are related. Helen does not strike me as too stupid to see it and honestly appears to be the kind of person who keeps her mouth shut until she has all the facts."

"How will you explain it to her, sir?"

"I wish I knew. I have no idea how to broach the subject with Simone, let alone explain how she did not recognize me to her friend, or how we have a child together. This is a fucking mess."

"I'm sorry sir. You don't deserve this."

"You should have seen her smile," Isaac whispers as he looks up at Jim with tortured eyes. "When I asked her why she named him Malik, she said it reminded her of his father and the child is all she has of him. The name means Master. I had to leave; her answer made me angry."

"Doesn't sound like a woman who will be upset with you to me, sir. Her husband did explain it was clear she knew it was all his fault. Maybe she doesn't blame you."

They both fall into silence after that, and Isaac considers all the possibilities of what could happen when he tells her. He knows she's not sure of him now, but she doesn't fear him. Well, except for that moment in the car, when he had failed to reassure her that her family was safe and waiting for her at his house. He hasn't handled any of this the right way at all, but he doesn't want to let her go.

Truth is, no matter how he looks at it, he doesn't deserve her. Not even though he thinks she's the most beautiful, smart, resilient, and amazing woman he's ever met. It doesn't matter that he hadn't known she wasn't a willing participant from the beginning or anything; in reality, he raped her.

The disgusting thought makes him want to puke, hating himself. He's unsure he'll ever not feel sick at wondering what things he did to her that she truly hadn't wanted. She hadn't even known the fucking safe word, which made it that much fucking worse. Now, all his memories of his time with her, feeling as if they connected in a way he hasn't ever connected with anyone before, they are all tainted. If she finds out and hates him, he won't be able to blame her. He will have to let her and his child walk out of his life, because he screwed up, and there's no denying it. To do so wouldn't be fair to her or how she feels.

Jim turns to leave the room, walking to the door and opening it before saying over his shoulder, "All you can do is tell her, sir. But perhaps wait until she is well enough to leave and take care of herself, if that's what she chooses. I'll see you in the morning."

Isaac sighs, knowing Jim is right, and wondering how the hell he is going to say nothing for the next few weeks. How he will keep his hands off, both her and their child, because he has no right to them at this point. Standing up, he shuts off the light and closes the office door, then heads up the steps.

His feet take him to her without him even thinking about it.

His Cara.

She is sleeping so peacefully as he stands there looking down at her, aching to touch her, kiss her, and hold her. He wishes he could just climb in bed and take her into his arms. Especially since he's the reason she's stuck in bed for now.

He hasn't slept so well since he took her home originally. Near the end, he stayed away from her because he fought his feelings for her. He knew he had to let her go home; after all, at the time, he had no idea what was going on. She had been her husbands, and he respected that. He couldn't just send her home without saying goodbye though.

And that's when he gave in to the urge to see how much she could take.

Big mistake.

He hit her with that belt, and god, she'd handled it beautifully. Letting her go home to what he thought a happy home had been his job, but turns out, she became the last job he took.

After his last disastrous and very public relationship, retreating from the world became his salvation. Fulfilling fantasies had been a way to get what he needed without the attachment. He hadn't needed the money and still didn't.

Which is why after she showed him there was a woman out there who might be willing to be what he needed, he stopped offering those services immediately.

However, she's all he's been able to think about since he saw her again, because she's perfect for him.

Worse is he knows how bad it is that he stalked her. He tracked her down, he knew all about her life before she saw him that first time, and she never had a chance to avoid him. He orchestrated every single moment since the night he gave her the more than average tip.

He knows every fucking inch of her. She might be filled out more now since having Malik, but god, it only enhances her beauty. He can't wait to see her naked again, feel her underneath him, and fuck her hard and deep like it will be the last time he fucks her.

She deserves better, and he knows it, but it doesn't matter because he wants her and only her.

He should've told her the truth from the beginning, because it would've been the right thing to do. And he's not a bad man; at least that's what he tells himself.

But if he were a good man, he wouldn't have presumed to know what's right and taken her out of her life that was 'all her own' as she said in the car. He would've sat her down and started their new relationship out honestly. He would do it tomorrow instead of waiting. He wouldn't be standing in her room, looking down at her, wishing he could wrap his fingers around his cock and jerk off right this instant as he stands above her.

He wouldn't have to hold his breath as she turns her head toward where he's standing next to the bed, eyes closed, and smiles as she whispers, "Master." A breath he releases as he takes an involuntarily step back, only to be halted by her next sound, a pain filled whimper. He knows she's still sleeping, probably deeply, but she is dreaming about him, and his gaze drops to the bed as she mumbles, "I'm cold. Please."

Isaac knows he shouldn't do it. He needs to walk out, but he doesn't want to. He wants to stay. He wants to hold her, reassure her even in her sleep, and god, he just wants to fucking touch her. Almost in a trance, he slips out of his shoes and his jacket, then his shirt and pants, and gently climbs in next to her in nothing but his boxers.

He's barely under the blankets and slipping his arm under her neck before she's wiggling back against him, snuggling into his body and warmth as if it's everything she sought in her dreams. With little hesitance, he wraps his arm around her waist, and for the first time in months, falls sound asleep quick.

SIMONE

I'm so sure it's a dream at first.

It's been so long since anyone has been in a bed with me, I figure the hand between my legs has to mean I'm dreaming. And not just on the outside either. The hand's inside my underwear, a single finger slipping between my labia, going back and forth gently over my clit.

Almost involuntarily, my body thrusts up a little, encouraging the hand, and with it comes a deep groan from behind me near my ear. The sound reminds me of Master when something I did pleased him, and I do it again, which results in him pushing my lower body back toward his. And there is his cock, hard against my ass, and I want to whimper with need.

I haven't had sex in a while so even if it's in a dream, I want to take advantage of it. But I know better than to ask, than to say anything, because he'll give me what I need when he wants to give it to me. At least, I think that at first, but this is my dream, and so I decide I'm going to do whatever it takes to make him give me what I want.

Using my right hand, I slip it down until it is underneath my bottoms as well, covering his hand, and I move my ass against him at the same time. My hand curls around his and I give a little pressure, letting him know I want him to touch me harder, and he slips another finger to join the first. Then they slip down until they are entering my pussy a little and I gasp with delight. I'm so wet, something that only happens when I think of him, and I know this will be everything I've been missing and more.

Over a year since I orgasmed last. No matter how hard I tried, mentally I couldn't, because I got used to him telling me to, or having to ask. I cried so hard after a while, because I thought I would go without orgasms forever if I never saw him again. But now, my body quickly approaches one as he slips his two fingers in deep and curls them to rub me just right.

"Oh god." The low-spoken words tumble out of my mouth as I move in time with his hand, my mind in a completely different place than my body as I go right back to the dark room where he put his hands on me best, pleading in a desperate whisper as his hand increases speed, "May I come Master? Please, let me come for you."

His mouth is on my neck, biting and sucking,

his cock trapped between our bodies, being rubbed in time with the movement of my hips against his hand. He doesn't answer as his hand strokes me faster and firmer, his thumb coming to rest on my clit but not moving, and even though I'm trying to hold off, I sob, "Fuck. Please, Master."

I think it's all a dream but apparently even in them, my body refuses to obey without his permission, and I'm about to beg again when he kisses the nape of neck, humming a clear, "Mhmm," in response. He tightens his grip so I feel every inch of him behind me in the crack of my ass as he flicks his thumb over my clit and my body tips over the edge of heaven in his arms.

Floating, it's almost with an otherworldly experience that I feel him move a little, his hand moving from between my legs to pulling down my underwear, and he doesn't even get them all the way off before he adjusts my hips a little so he can fuck me perfectly from behind. The tip of his cock probes my entrance, and I nearly sob with joy as the tip slides in. He's so big, and in this position it's so tight, every inch feels delicious and like agony all at once. His hand comes across my front to slip between my legs again, giving him the perfect way to go as slow as he likes, and increase the pressure in order to keep our lower bodies locked together.

The moment I realize this is real happens

when he groans and finally thrusts hard, making my body take him all at once...and my chest explodes with pain at the sudden hard movement as I become completely alert.

This time my words are not in pleasure but in pain as my eyes fly open, the words loud and abrupt into the darkness. "Oh god. Stop! Stop!"

I'm awake, but it's clear Isaac's not as his sigh of contentment coincides with his hand cupping me harder between the legs, and he pulls out of me until he's near the edge before plunging back in as hard as before.

Tears spring to my eyes, but only because of the pain shooting through my chest, totally killing any enjoyment him fucking me would bring. This isn't how I thought my first time with Isaac would be the few times I've seriously considered it, and I lift my hand in a panic because I just want him to wake up and be gentler, even though I don't understand how he ended up in bed with me in the first place.

"Quit!" I say in a loud voice, bringing my hand back and slapping blindly in the dark at his body, as he does the same action once again and the pain intensifies. "Oooh, fuck. Ow, ow, ow."

I'm afraid to wake the house but as he prepares to do it again, I give in and scream a little louder while reaching behind me to smack at something, anything. "Isaac! Wake up!"

He jumps, his body jerking out of and away

from mine as I burst into sobs, feeling him exit the bed with a confused, "What?" After a moment, I feel the bed dip, and he puts his hand on my arm, his words still thick with sleep. "Simone? Did I hurt you?"

"Not on purpose," I manage to get out between sobs. "Thought it was... a dream...at first."

"Fuck's sake," he grinds out as he removes his hand from touching me. "I should not have gotten into bed with you. I apologize. It is clear I need to stay away from you because I keep hurting you."

I take a deep shuddering breath, letting it out slow and steady to calm myself, and then say in a near whisper, "Please don't. It wasn't your fault—"

"Oh yes it is," he interrupts, leaving the bed again as if I hadn't just asked him to stay, and making me feel like I've done something wrong. "You asked me stay; I knew you were most likely not aware of what you asked and should have left, not climbed in bed next to you."

"You just thrust a bit hard with your dick, Isaac, not beat me in your sleep." My words are filled with irritation and sarcasm, the pain in my chest subsiding a little as I calm down. "Seriously, don't turn this into a big deal."

I can't see him, but I hear him growl before he says in a soft voice, "Do you even hear yourself right this instant? I just 'thrust a bit hard with my dick'? My dick should not have been in you to begin with!"

My voice sounds so small, I hate it, but his words make my eyes fill with tears. "It was nice at first. Don't be mad, please." I reach back enough to pat the bed but not hurt myself again, and say, "Please, come back to bed."

"Simone, you are in no position to—" He cuts off as I start crying and seconds later I feel him sit next to me on the bed. "Please, no crying. I did not mean to upset you. I simply do not wish to hurt you again."

"Maybe you should ask what I want for once instead," I snap at him, rolling over slowly onto my back to face him even though it's too dark to see anything, something I'm glad for since I'm sure the tears have made my face all splotchy. "You just shove your way into my life and climb into my bed without my permission." Okay, that's not entirely true but he's pissing me off. "Then you go and fucking apologize for it. Either be an asshole or don't be one, but pick a fucking side before you shove your cock into me again!"

"Eight," is all he says.

"Screw you, Isaac. I'd say since I'm laying in this bed, in your house, in lots of pain due to you scaring the shit out of me makes us even, as *this* is most definitely your fault."

Instead of retorting, I feel him move until he's crouching over me. My body instantly reawakens as my mind registers our close proximity, wanting to continue with our activities earlier. One hand is next to my head, palm against the bed supporting his weight, as the other cups my cheek. I wish he would at least put a little weight on me, as his over carefulness is pissing me off a little, but instead he leans down and covers my mouth with his.

"Fucking you is not an option," he says against my lips after a few deep kisses. "Gentle is not something I do and you are in no position to give it to me how I like it." His land leaves my face and slips between our bodies as he instructs, "Lift your shirt as high as you can get it."

I do as he says, sliding my shirt up near my neck as I ask, "Why?"

"Because." He moves his mouth away from mine and into the crook of my neck as I feel him let out a hiss. "I am going to be an asshole and come all over your breasts, as the thought of going to jerk off in the shower when you are right here seems a bit rude."

What else can I do but laugh at his honesty? And I'd rather he use my body than leave me right now.

"Will you at least kiss me while you do it?"

He brings his body down enough I can feel his cock against my stomach, his hand around it, and instead of answering, moves his head back up until our lips are close enough to touch. "Yes, but if I am hurting you, just slap me on the arm because once I put my mouth on yours, it is not likely I will release it until the end."

"Okay."

His lips touch mine, but then he pulls back to murmur, "Did you at least come earlier?"

My face heats at the memory of how hard I came against his hand fucking me even though he can't see me, and I manage to squeak out, "Yes, thank you."

I feel him smile against my mouth as he says, "Good. Put your arms around my neck. I want your hands on me during this."

Bringing my arms up from where they rest on the bed, I put one on each bare shoulder, sliding them in toward his neck, and then around until I feel like I'm holding on for dear life. My fingers move up and tangle in his hair as his mouth finally takes mine under his, his tongue thrusting in hard and fast like his cock had earlier. I feel his hand move between us, his hips moving in rhythm with the strokes of his hand as he pleasures himself, and I'm jealous of his hand. I want him to be moving like that inside me, because even though my chest hurt, the feeling of having him in me had been amazing.

I'm so frustrated with the way he's fucking my mouth with his, and fucking his cock with his hand, like I want him to be doing it to me that my hands tighten on his hair with my dissatisfaction. He groans into my mouth, his hand speeding up to the point I'm amazed he isn't setting us on fire with the friction, his body thrusting harder into his own hand which presses on my stomach anyway, until I wonder why I didn't just let him fuck me even if it did hurt.

Why I wish for such a thing, I don't know, but all I know is…I want to be consumed by this man. I don't know why he picked me, I don't like the way he pushed himself into my life, but now here he is. He's in this bed with me, pleasuring himself while in my arms, and strangely enough in this moment I finally get him, at least a little. He is like the person I've become and for once, I don't feel so alone.

He growls, bringing my attention back to him at the same time he moves enough to catch my lower lip between his teeth, nipping it as he thrusts one final time. I feel his come splash onto my breasts and stomach once, twice, as he moans long and hard into my mouth. When he stops moving, he gives me a final deep french kiss, then rolls away and off the bed.

"I will be right back, going to get something to clean up."

I don't say anything since I don't need to. He doesn't go far, as there is a bathroom connected to my room, and he's back in a flash with a wet washcloth. He wipes me off, then himself before taking it back, and returns quick to slide into bed next to me.

When I'm snuggled into his arms like I was when I first woke up, I feel relaxed enough to say, "Isaac? May I ask you something?"

"Hmm? Sure."

"Why do you prefer the darkness?"

"Well, you go right for the jugular." His chuckle is soft as he presses a kiss to my shoulder and says after a few moments, "I used to live in the light. I did not like my experience with it. The light hides so much even though it feels as if one should be able to see everything. The darkness has no such expectations. We do not expect to see anything in the dark, but it has its own way of making you examine yourself even when you do not want to, makes you feel perhaps even when you would rather not." He sighs, relaxing behind me. "Does that answer your question sufficiently?"

"Yes."

And it does, because I know exactly what he means. My life in the light with my husband had ended up being a lie. And what I had in the dark those two months? I felt all wrong for feeling as I had, but something in me knew Master had been a good person, which is why I fell in love with him anyway. Never once did I fear him, never once did I hate him because deep down, I saw him with my heart in a way my eyes had never gotten to.

I know it would never make sense to anyone in the light of day, and perhaps that is why I've never said a word. And for a second, I wonder if I told

Isaac, what he would think, but I don't want to risk it. Not even as we lie here in the dark because I can't be sure of his reaction.

Instead, I close my eyes and fall asleep, content in his arms and the way he makes me feel even if I still don't know why he wants me.

11

ISAAC

A WHOLE WEEK HAS PASSED, yet Isaac still can't believe he fucked Simone as he slept. However, he had thought it a dream as much as she had, and waking up to her panicked slap had made him feel like the asshole she'd called him.

He continues to feel like an asshole even now, because all he can think about is bending her over and fucking her so hard and fast, until they both are desperate for air. Being unable to touch her until she heals completely makes it so he can't even be in the same room as her as much as he wishes to, and he's afraid she'll start to believe he's avoiding her.

He's not, but fuck, he can't even think about her without his cock going rock hard, as it is in this instant.

Especially since she's lying in bed right now sound asleep, moaning in her sleep while saying, 'Master' over and over. It's making him think about every single moment he spent in that dark room with her, every moan and sigh he wrung from her body time and again, and how fucking badly he wishes he could do it right now.

Instead, he's relegated to sitting in a chair in her room, watching her at night when she doesn't know he's here, fucking his hand with his dick because he can't thrust it deep inside her hot pussy.

His pussy, at that.

Yes, his, because every inch of her belongs to him, and he can't wait for her to know who he is, for her to acknowledge all the ways he owns her. Every day she spends here, every second he's around her and their child, the more he admits to himself there isn't a chance in fucking hell she's walking out of his life.

Because while he considers himself a good guy, she's the only person in a long time to make him feel anything, and there's no way he's letting someone like that go. He may not deserve her, but if he has to, he will ask her what he needs to do for her to feel as if she belongs to him, and he'll fucking do it.

That is, only if her answer doesn't include letting her leave, because such a thing will not be happening.

He steps closer to the bed, reaching out and taking a small piece of the blanket covering her body in-between two fingers, and slowly pulling it down to expose her bare skin to the air.

The reason for her choice to sleep nude is unclear to him, and he obviously can't ask, but he loves her decision to do so following that night.

Maybe she hopes he'll come back and climb into bed with her again, but it's not something he can allow to happen again. There's no way to control the situation, and the desire to fuck her overrules all common sense he possesses when her naked body is up against his.

But right now?

Well, right now he's going do what he's been doing every night for a week: he's going to touch her and come all over her lovely fucking breasts while she sleeps.

He's never met such a sound sleeper in his life, and he's not ashamed to admit he's taking blatant advantage of it. Sure, he could lock himself in his office and watch videos of their time together — thank fuck for night vision cameras — all those months ago, stroke himself to the visual and the memories, but why bother when the real version lie naked and bathed in moonlight right in front of his eyes?

Even as he takes himself in hand, stroking slow and steady, thinking about the stuff he has on video makes him feel the tiniest bit of guilt about not knowing the situation at the time. However, he quickly tamps it down and shoves it to the side because there's nothing he can do about it now, and he'll more than make it up to her for the rest of their lives together.

When it's them together, when she's calling him by his real name in the outside world and 'Master' in the bedroom, that's the time he can't wait for. He wants to fuck her every way imaginable, sink her back down to his level of darkness, and surprisingly, see her pregnant with his children.

A soft whimper drags his thoughts away from anything less than pure carnality, and he only waits a breath before cupping her breast in his free hand, giving it a rough squeeze. When she moans, his cock jumps in his hand, and he hisses as he clasps his cock tighter.

He sucks in a breath when she lifts both of her arms, grinning into the near darkness as she moves them above her head on the pillow, and leaves them there. Her submission even in her sleep pleases him. Bending over, he pumps his cock harder and faster as he takes a nipple in his mouth, sucking and biting it until it's a hard bud, and releases it with a pop.

It's when he looks up, seeing her with her eyes closed, her chest rising slow and steady, and her mouth open enough the simple thought of putting his cock in it has him moving up the side of the bed. Knowing he shouldn't, he simply can't resist temptation, and decides to do it for just a few moments.

Her position near the edge of it is perfect, making him only have to lean in a bit to rub the tip of his cock around the rim of her lips, and for good measure to test how deep asleep she is, he taps her cheek with it. When he gets no response, he goes back to running his cock around her lips, only to groan when her tongue innocently darts out to wet them and catches the tip on the way.

Controlling the instant urge to shove his way into her mouth, he moves so his cock is pressing down on her tongue, then slowly begins inserting it into her mouth, sliding along her tongue until the tip is past her lips. He pauses as she tries to close her mouth, which has the added effect of almost sucking, and once again he has to control the urge to thrust.

It's hard not to as he remembers the way she took his cock in her mouth and to the back of her throat like a pro before. Sure, it had taken some work to get there, but god, she'd been the best cocksucker he'd ever dealt with by the end.

And now it seems like her body recalls what to do, because she relaxes her mouth and throat, her body going limp as she sighs. He's a goner then, knowing he's not going to remove his cock from between her luscious lips until he's come long and hard down her throat.

Using both hands to steady her head with his hands clasped tightly in her hair, she moans around his dick as he moves it further and further inside her mouth, a soft groan of his own escaping when he's in as far as possible. He keeps it there, relishing the rapid swallowing of her throat around his tip, her tongue trying to move along his length but not being able to, the way her hands clasp and unclasp as they lie above her head as she forces herself to keep them where they are, and god, he wishes she would hear his praises if he were to say any.

"God yes," he hisses between clenched teeth as he retreats and shoves forward again, the slight raking of her teeth along his length rounded off with her immediate swallowing to try to rid her throat of the offending object.

For several minutes, the only sounds are those he makes as he moves in and out, over and over, her occasional whimper or sigh encouraging him. He fears her waking up, yet the desire to mark her as his even if he's the only one aware overtakes anything else.

Soon, he's holding her head completely still, his cock lodged deep in her mouth as he shoots his load down the back of her throat while swallowing his own deep groan of contentment and pleasure as her own throat works.

He pulls out with a pop, quickly backing away into the shadows while shoving himself back into his pants as she coughs once, and then sighs with relief as he hears her licking her lips.

Nothing can prevent the naughty grin on his face as he turns toward the door and leaves as quietly as he arrived, looking forward to the day when he can do that while she's wide awake and on her knees.

A day which comes sooner than either of them possibly expected.

SIMONE

NEARLY TWO WEEKS passed before I got fed up with sitting or lying still all the time. It hadn't taken much to convince Isaac I needed to be up and moving around, not to mention give my son way more attention than he'd been getting from me. So that meant we all spent a lot of time together because it's not like Isaac or I left the house to work. Since it's been cold outside, whenever Malik slept, Isaac and I would watch t.v. or a movie, or just play a card game with Helen and sometimes Jim.

And now today is three weeks since I came here to his house, and the doctor has cleared me. Shocked though he was that I healed so quickly, it's nice to be free to do whatever I want.

I know what Isaac wants to do. Me. But, contrary to what I thought he would do after the night he stayed in my room, he's kept away. He hasn't snuck into bed with me again, and seems to avoid me other than when we spend time together during the day, to the point I don't know whether to be amused or insulted.

We are sitting in the living room. Helen is helping make lunch, I'm reading a book in a comfy chair, and Isaac sits on the floor playing with Malik. Well, kind of. It's mostly Malik sitting up with the assistance of Isaac's hands. Each of Malik's little hands are wrapped around the index finger on each one of Isaac's, his chubby little cheeks smiling with delight.

It's weird, honestly, seeing them next to one another. Malik is so tiny, and Isaac is so big. But Helen hadn't been exaggerating about how much everyone here loves Malik, and I've only seen him wrap them tighter around his little fingers the longer we've been here. And how could he not? He's a happy little ham.

What's really great is seeing Isaac interact with Malik. I've not been around many other people, but even my own father didn't pay me as much attention as Isaac does to my son. If he's around, he holds Malik, not me or Helen. A few times I've caught Helen eyeing him carefully, looking deep in thought, and every time I ask her what she's staring at him so intently for, she just laughs and says it's just sweet how he is with the baby.

"Whoops," Isaac says, and I look up at them just as Malik starts to fall back toward the floor, one of his arms flailing in the air.

Isaac is quick, his hand swooping in to cover the back of Malik's head along with the other stopping his fall, and then helps the baby to lie flat. Malik starts coo'ing and kicking while waving his arms around and Isaac bends over him so he's staring him the face. Malik giggles as Isaac's hair falls around his face, and he swipes for it, catching the strands in his fist to tug on.

Chuckling, Isaac manages to free his hair from my son's grip, and I see him reach over for the little extra blanket nearby. He covers his eyes up with it, and after a few seconds says, "Peek-a-boo!" Pulling it away, Malik looks stunned for a second, then starts giggling once more. Isaac does it a few more times, and each time, Malik giggles a little louder and longer.

After the last time, I see him lean in and kiss Malik on the cheek, then pull back and stick the blanket against his mouth.

And that's when it happens. That's when my whole world as I know it falls apart.

Because Isaac says something, but I don't register the words coming out of his mouth. I only hear the muffled voice coming from behind the blanket. Maybe I gasp at the moment I recognize it's him, maybe I make a noise, I don't know; but Isaac's gaze goes from Malik's to mine in confusion.

"You bastard," I whisper as I stand, my gaze flicking between him and my son — correction, *our son* — as my whole body starts to shake. "You fucking son of a bitch."

His eyes round in horror as he looks down at the blanket, which he then tosses to the side before standing, his mouth flattening in a grim line as he realizes he just ratted himself out with the innocent piece of fabric. "I can explain—"

"Fuck you," I hiss while taking a step toward him. "Get out of my way and give me my baby."

"I believe you are referring to *our* child, correct?"

I take another step because I want my baby, pointing a finger at him, not caring how crazy I seem right now. I just want to get Malik, leave the room, and wrap my head around this. "I swear, if you don't get the fuck out of my way, I'll—"

His eyes glitter as he advances on me, grasping me by my upper arms before I can run, and lifting a little off the ground as he puts his face real close to mine. "What will you do, hmm? Slap me? Kick me? You can do it later if you wish. We will not have it out in front of my staff or where they can hear us. But I will allow you to say your piece."

Even if his words pierced my bubble of disbelief and anger, I'm not given the chance to respond due to the arrival of Helen.

"Um, what the hell is going on here?"

Both our heads swing her way; his face going neutral as I burst into tears. He continues to leave me dangling in the air as he addresses her.

"Helen, Simone and I need to go have a long, private discussion. Would you please watch our son?"

Through my tears I watch her take in what he's said, nodding after a moment before announcing with a soft laugh and a face filled with confusion, "I knew it. But—"

"Please," he says while tossing me over his shoulder, cutting off her next obvious question, and any comments from me with a warning squeeze on my leg. "Not right now."

He doesn't even wait for her reply, carrying me out of the room like I'm a sack of potatoes, pissing me off every second he treats me this way.

I'd ask myself who the fuck he thinks he is, but we both know who he is.

Grr. Who he was.

I can't believe he didn't tell me.

Well, yes, I guess I can. Because he's an asshole. And I want him to know what I think.

"You're a fucking asshole." I lift my hands and fist them, hitting him in the middle of his back. "Put me down, right now!"

He smacks me hard on my ass, making me yelp with the shock of it, hissing, "What did I say? Shut up until we are alone unless you wish for everyone to know your business."

"Mine?" I laugh, loudly, since that happens to be the funniest thing I've heard in a while. "What about your fucking business? My god, you specialized in—"

Stopping abruptly in the middle of the hallway, he yanks my body down until I'm in front of him, but my feet still don't touch the floor as he holds me to his body with one strong arm. His face is thunderous as the other arm comes up and he covers my mouth with his palm.

"I swear, I will fucking gag you if you do not shut up right now. Until we are in the soundproof room, if you say another word, you will not get to say your piece. Instead you will find yourself chained to the bed you ought to remember well with my dick down your throat, got it?"

It's too bad, it really is, since I love everything about his cock. But I'm pissed, and his words don't scare me, so in a fit of pique and to show him two people can play this game, I move my leg back, hauling off and kicking him with my leather boot-covered foot, which catches him right in the knee.

Okay, so I hurt myself more than him because he's built and muscled, but the hiss that flows of his mouth and the look of utter astonishment on his face is enough. Not to mention it makes him off guard enough I move my mouth and bite his hand.

"Dammit!"

His grip lessens enough I push off and slip out of his grasp while thanking nature for my small size in my head, and even though I hit the floor, I recover first as I scramble to my feet and take off running.

I'm not an idiot, I know he'll catch me, especially because I haven't gone through the house much. I'm not sure where I'm going and the last thing he wants to be seen doing is chasing me. I hear his footfalls behind me, getting closer and closer, until finally he snatches me around my waist just as I'm about to turn another corner.

I won't scream though. I don't want to get him in trouble, but I do want to make him pay for keeping his identity a secret from me. But he chuckles as he tosses me over his shoulder once more and I go limp, tired from exerting myself after so many weeks of not really doing anything.

"Good girl," he praises as he slaps me on the ass. "You led us right to the door which leads to the basement. What an excellent memory you have."

See, if I wasn't so mad, I would laugh because we both know I never knew where I was kept, or how to get there. And because I refuse to just give up totally right now, I respond with a whispered, "Fuck you."

"That is seven." He opens the door and I feel him reach into his pocket where I know his phone is. He hits a button and puts the phone up to his ear as he asks, "Want to go for an even ten?"

"The fuck it is."

"Eight. And yes it is. I am counting bastard since calling me such was unnecessary as my parents were married." My mouth drops open at that as he clears his throat and steps inside the door while saying into his phone, "Bring the papers to the room." He pauses, then follows it up with, "Yes. Thank you."

He turns to close the door behind us just as I glimpse the spiral stars, making me whimper as it goes dark all around us, afraid he'll trip and kill us both. But the second the door shuts, little lights illuminate along the floor, similar to how they work in an airplane, and he doesn't say another word to me as he carries me down the steps. When we reach the bottom, he stops, and I hear him pull out keys, the sound of him inserting one into a lock reaching my ears within a second.

Stepping inside, he kicks the door shut and walks us down a long hallway until he stops, opens another, and walks into complete darkness, the door closing behind us all on its own.

"Look at this," he goads with a dark chuckle as he slides me down until my feet touch the floor. "Home sweet home, gorgeous. What do you think? Does it look the same?"

"You know damn well I can't see a fucking thing," I say as I shove against him with both hands once he lets me go, the room so dark I can't even see the outline of his body. Oh yes, I remember this room all too well as I snap at him before he can say anything to me. "Yes, yes, I know. *Nine*."

He doesn't immediately react to what I've said, or to the fact I pushed him with my hands; instead I feel his hand come up to cup my cheek. His thumb strokes it before moving to my lips and rubbing across them. Then he moves the hand to the back of my head. I feel the blunt tips of his nails scratch lightly against my scalp as he claws my hair in his hand, gaining a solid hold on it as he tugs my head back, baring my neck at the same time he moves to overpower me.

Before long, the pressure has my knees buckling, and he doesn't let go even when I'm on my knees on the tile floor. I feel him crouch down in front of me, his other hand coming up to my hair to pull out my tie, which sets it free. The hand clawing my hair lets go and it cascades down my back, but my freedom doesn't last long. He traps me in his grasp with a hand on each side of my head, re-tangling his fingers in it as he tips my head back a little, and presses his lips against my mouth. He doesn't seek entrance into my mouth with the gentle persuasion I've become used to; he demands it with a hard thrust of his tongue.

I've no idea how we stay balanced in this position as he devours my mouth with his, stealing all my breath as the kiss goes on and on, our tongues engaging in a fight only he has a chance of winning. His assault on my senses is relentless, his hold on my head unrelenting, and every whimper or moan of pleasure is stolen from me before it even has a chance to go anywhere else.

The knock at the door is what makes him pull away abruptly, releasing me gently as he says, "When I come back, I expect you to be in my favorite position wearing absolutely nothing."

I sit frozen, remembering with clarity the position he wants to find me in, as I see a sliver of light come through when he opens the door. He slips out, shutting the door behind him, and I scramble up to do as he bids.

Because even now — no, especially now — I've no desire to learn what the consequences for not listening are.

It's bad enough I've no idea what he'll do for my outburst earlier, even though he completely deserved it; I also know he doesn't like when I swear outside of the bedroom. I know I'm going to find out, after he lets me ask my questions, and I have so fucking many.

As I strip, they run through my mind. Why let me go if he was just going to come after me? Did he know I hadn't consented? If he does know, is he afraid I'll tell? Also if he knows, is that why he didn't tell me who he was? Did he want me to know him as Isaac so I could see he isn't a bad man? Did he intend to tell me at all? Had he done all this to simply make sure I'm okay or does he want more? If he does, where do we go from here?

Most of all, does he love me?

What does it mean for me and Malik if he doesn't?

Maybe it's crazy to think this, but everything I've seen so far shows me he doesn't intend to let me go again. He told me in the car on the way here I'm meant for him, and he's going to make me his.

And it's this thought that makes me smile because I wonder how long I can torture him, making him wonder whether I want him or not, before telling him what I actually feel.

Because I fell in love with a faceless man who made me feel everything in the dark, and now I've seen his face in the light. All I want to do is tell him, but first, he deserves to pay for deceiving me. I'm not the same girl who came into this room that first time, nor am I the same woman who left. If I end up in the dark again, it's because I want to be willing, not because he thinks he can do whatever he wants.

The door starts to open, startling me from my thoughts, and tossing my panties to the side, I get back on my knees. Then, straightening my back and jutting my breasts out, I put my hands behind my back, palms up with one hand on top of the other. And just in time too, because he finishes walking in, stops to look at me while the light blinds me enough I turn my head to the side to avoid it, and then shuts the door softly behind him.

When he speaks, his voice is smooth and deep, filled with a desire and affection that is like long-forgotten music to my ears, my heart soaring as he says the words I never thought I'd hear again.

"Hello, Cara."

ISAAC

ISAAC STANDS INSIDE THE DOOR, relishing the brief glimpse he's just had of the woman he wants more than anything else in the world kneeling naked on the floor, her subservience to him even in her anger telling him everything he needs to know.

He won't make Simone stay that way long; he doesn't really have the right to at this point.

When he commanded her to do it, he merely wanted to see if she were willing, or if she would remain defiant. And her willingness is immensely pleasing in more ways than one.

Maybe this won't be the disaster he's feared it would be for months now.

And thank fuck everything is in the open now. He has grown tired of hiding it from her and not being able to call Malik his own.

Now he can.

Carefully weighing his options, he decides the

best way to begin to handle how they came to know each other the first time, and how they know each other now, is to start back where they were and figure out how to integrate them with her. Together.

"Hello, Cara," he says, walking forward until he is able to rest his hand on the top of her head, the other hand carrying the papers Jim brought him, and stops. "You may sit down and relax. You may not speak. Yet."

She says nothing, simply sighing and rearranging herself so she sits on the ground, his hand on her head the whole time.

God, she is fucking beautiful, and perfect. And all his.

The corner of his lips curl up at his thoughts while he simply stands above her, relishing this moment as long as he can, because he has been waiting what feels like an eternity for it to arrive.

And he wants to skip this unpleasantness. He doesn't want to worry she will walk out the door and take their child with her, and tell him to fuck off. He knows he would deserve it, but it is not what he wants, not at all.

He wants her. Next to him, under him, everywhere; as long as she is his.

Since the morning he awakened with his dick deep inside her, he tried to keep his distance and failed. He learned no single part of his body wished to cooperate with his plans; not his heart, not his cock, and not his hands. Nothing. Every single fiber of his being made it impossible to stay away from her at all while she healed, much as he'd known he needed to behave the whole time.

Yes, he wanted to fuck her once before telling her who he really was, even if it wouldn't have been the right thing to do. He can't believe he screwed up and put the blanket against his mouth. Truth is, he let his guard down; for a moment he'd forgotten who they were to each other and hadn't thought his actions through.

For as long as he lives though, he will never forget the look on her face when she realized he was her Master; the unconscious look of longing on her face coinciding with the affection in her gaze, which had been quickly replaced by the look of horror at realizing his deception.

Now she sits in the dark room, waiting for him to speak. All he wants to do is put her on the bed and fuck her until she sobs with pleasure, and hopefully forgets at the same time why she's in this room once more.

But first comes something he needs to do, that needs said, and he fears it will upset her even more.

Isaac moves until he's standing in front of her and lowers his body until he's on his knees facing her. She can't see him and he can't see her, but that doesn't matter. Dropping the papers to the floor next to him, he lifts both hands and places them on her bare shoulders, feeling her deep inhalation of breath as he does so.

Her smooth skin is hot against his palms, and for a moment, he merely enjoys the simple act of touching her. She doesn't move, and he wonders what she's thinking, feeling. He knows she undressed as he asked, is in position as he asked, and hasn't spoken because he told her not to. These are all things she's giving him freely, yet he wonders when it will change, when she will demand her due because of his deception.

She relaxes beneath his touch, letting out a soft sigh in the continued silence, and he finally forces what he needs to say past his lips. As a man of honor and a Master, an apology is necessary, and something which must be given since he wronged her, even unknowingly.

"I wish to apologize." As she stiffens beneath his touch, he wishes he could slide his hands up and into her hair, caress her face, reassure her with his touch, but knows he doesn't have the right to at this point. "When you arrived initially, I had no idea you were unaware of what your husband had done. I never would have touched you."

She remains silent as he commanded her, so he continues, getting it all out so she knows exactly what happened up until this point. "I never expected to see you again, and there you were in the restaurant one night, far away from where I knew you lived. I followed you home, tracking down your husband once I realized you lived in that apartment alone, and after he told me what he had done, I kicked his fucking ass."

She gasps, but he keeps speaking. "His actions sickened me. He turned something beautiful, something I did for myself and my clients out of pure mutual enjoyment, into something dirty and, quite frankly, criminal. I was so disgusted by what he had done, and in turn I had done, I almost turned myself in, but then I knew I would not be able to make it up to you. You were in your situation because of him, and I had the power to do everything I could to make it up to you."

It's then she cuts in, breaking the rules with a whispered question, filled with clear confusion and a slight wavering that gives away her emotions. "Why didn't you just tell me?"

He moves his right hand, sliding it toward her neck, dipping into the curve before gliding up and around until he can slip his hand into her hair. She shivers a little as his fingers steal through it, where he ends up enclosing some of it in his fist, and tugs her head back a little bit. He can't help himself even though he knows he should keep his hands off her like this until they've come to an agreement.

But his body responds, his cock hardening and straining against its confinement as an involuntary moan slips through her lips, and he moves his other hand. Gliding it down her arm by trailing his blunt nails against her skin, he goes all the way to the tips of her fingers before relocating his hand to the underside of her breast, cupping it in his palm. She moans, the sound of her pleasure mixing with a whimper as he pinches the nipple between his thumb and index finger hard, and he has to force himself not to pick her up and throw her on the nearby bed.

"What do you imagine I should have said, hm?" He leans in, making sure his mouth is close enough to hers he may touch it if he wishes, and continues in a hushed yet harsh tone. "Something such as, 'Hi, I am the man who kept you in a dark room for two months and fucked you. And I would like to fuck you again'? I am sure that would have gone over well."

In a swift motion, he moves his hand to her other breast, pinching her nipple in the same hard manner as the other, making her cry out. And with one smooth action, he wraps his arm around her waist, then stands up while holding her against his body.

"Fuck this," he says, his voice gravelly with desire and need as he walks her over to the bed, easy to do in this dark room he's spent a lot of time in. "I have waited a long time for this. I do not wish to wait any longer to have you again."

Releasing his grip on her hair, he lowers her until she sits on the bed, and tells her as he unbuttons his shirt, "If you wish to stop, you need to tell me now."

Unable to see her, the absolute lack of noise in the room means he's attuned to the sound of her every breath, and he continues to undress as no objection is forthcoming. As he's shrugging off his shirt, he stills when her hands start unbuckling his belt. Letting the shirt drift to the floor, he clenches his hands into fists at his sides to keep from touching her, from making her stop what she's doing. Her touch is foreign, and other than all those weeks ago when he'd told her to put her arms around his neck, he hasn't been touched in a long time. Years, in truth.

He maintains his rigid stance because he doesn't want her to stop, especially as she tugs one side of the belt and starts to pull it through the loops. Then, when the belt is free, he only knows she drops it to the ground because the heavy buckle clangs on tile, and within a second her fingers are unbuttoning and unzipping his pants.

She tugs them enough to slip her hand inside and wrap her dainty hand around his cock, her breath hitching at the same time a hiss slips through his clenched teeth at the sensation. He knows from experience she's the perfect height as she sits on the edge of the bed for him to fuck her mouth with ease, and while wondering if she remembers that too, he also aches to shove his hands into her hair once again and take over.

But god, her hand on his cock is smooth and hot. She is not even able to enclose her whole hand around it, and when she gives his cock a squeeze right then, he groans softly as it flexes in response. His self-control hangs on a thread when her soft, wet tongue licks across the tip, before circling down and around the underside of the head, and that's when he can't hold back any longer.

His hands come up to her hair, spearing through it on each side of her head before fisting some in each hand, both of them moaning when she wraps her lips around him and ceases touching him. At that point, he thrusts into her mouth. The first two are shallow, but the warm invitation of her delicious mouth is too much to ignore, and after securing her head in a firm grip, he plunges deep into the back of her throat. His pleasure only heightens when he realizes she's relaxed her body to accept him, her arms having dropped to her sides, and smiles a wicked grin into the dark when the whimper she makes vibrates around every inch of him.

Every single time he pulls out, he enjoys the gasp of air she takes. Then, he counts to three in his head, flexing his grip in her hair on the third count to make sure she's secure before plunging back in, and relishes the feel of her lips closing around him. Her tongue occasionally swirls around the tip if she can manage it, her throat swallowing when she can't hold off any longer, and her moans when he moves his hips to push them both a little further excite him even more.

Fuck, he trained her well. She doesn't fight, she just takes what he gives her, and with an angry growl at remembering why she does so well, he uses her hair to forcefully yank her off him. As she falls to the bed with a soft cry, he shoves his dick back into his pants, and stalks over to the other side of the room.

"Cover your eyes," he says harsher than he intends to. "I am about to turn on a light."

"There's a fucking light in here?"

He almost laughs at the indignation in her voice, but instead says in the most asshole way he can, "That is ten. And I said, cover your fucking eyes. That was not permission to speak." He waits for a moment with his hand on the switch, then asks, "Ready?"

She remains silent and after turning his head the opposite direction, he turns on the lamp. It's not a harsh light, but he rapidly blinks a few times while his eyes quickly adjust, and looks over at her.

She's using the comforter as a shield, and after a few lowering and liftings of it, she puts it down and glares at him from where she sits on the bed with her legs crossed. "There was a lamp in here the whole time?"

Her anger makes him happy. After all, she

should be angry; she shouldn't be so accepting, it's going to get her in fucking trouble. But her ire brings a gorgeous flush to her face, her lips glistening and a deep pink from what they've just done, her hair wild and messy around her naked body from his hands, so all he wants to do is stalk back over and fuck her.

He doesn't do that though. Instead, he walks over to where the papers are on the ground, picks them up, and then goes to stand in front of her by the bed once more.

She isn't paying attention to him at all. Her eyes are all over the room she spent so much time in that isn't dark anymore, and he can see the fury building throughout her whole body as she takes in the contents. A lamp, a couch, a plush carpet on the other half of the room, a mini kitchen, and two cushy chairs — items she had no idea existed in this room because she'd only ever been on the bed and the tile floor surrounding it while here before.

"I spent a lot of time down here after you first arrived," he murmurs as she returns her temper-filled gaze back to his. "You would fall asleep after our time together, and I would sit in a chair with a drink to make sure you were okay. Sometimes for hours."

She looks at him then, the angry hardness of her gaze softening a little as she lifts a hand and grabs his free one, wrapping her fingers around his. She gives them a squeeze as he asks the one question he has to have the answer to.

"You did not fight me." He drops the papers on the bed beside her and lifts a hand to her cheek, cupping it in his palm as she intuitively tilts her face into it, her eyes fluttering closed. "Why did you accept your plight so easily?"

"I thought it was real," she breathes while keeping her eyes shut and her face in his hand. "I had no reason to believe anything else and I knew that fighting would probably only make things worse."

Although her answer doesn't surprise him, he does find it odd. Her reason is logical, but her reaction to being kidnapped and kept against her will should've been emotional; instinctual. She should've fought like hell, not thought logically about how giving in would be easier.

His voice is gruff when he speaks again, dropping his hands away from her face and swiping up the papers as she opens her eyes, staring at him with a questioning gaze. "I want you to look at these. They are the papers signed to ensure—"

"No." She shakes her head and looks away. "I don't wish to see them."

"You must. You need to see—"

"No!" Slapping at him, the papers fly out of his hand as she makes contact, and scrambles back on the bed away from him with a scowl. "I don't want to see. I don't care about the stupid fucking papers—"

Isaac, shocked at her angry reaction, curls his hands at the look on her face which he can't seem to decipher and clenches his jaw for a moment before stating in an even tone, "Eleven."

"Do something about it then." Back straight, her eyes flash at him with ill-concealed irritation, matching the deepening glare as she crosses her arms over her chest while rising onto her knees. "All you do is count. You've yet to punish me. What are you waiting for?"

Her brattiness amuses him while his body appreciates the view of her naked form in the light even though her breasts are obscured by her arms. However, instead of smiling as he wants to, he forces his gaze to stay neutral with his lips compressed in a thin line.

"Well?" She's taunting him, he realizes, which only makes his palm itch to smack her ass but he simply stands still as stone while she digs herself a bigger hole with her mouthy attitude. "I'm *fucking* waiting, *Isaac*, for you to fucking punish me."

They stare at one another, and for once in his life, he doesn't know where to go from here.

Yes, she's talking to him in a way nobody else would dare. Yes, she's not saying to let her go, or asking to leave the room.

So why doesn't he give her what she wants?

After all, he wants nothing more than to turn

her over his knee and spank her, but he admits to himself he doesn't want to punish her. At least, not in a way that doesn't also bring her pleasure because all he wants is to satisfy her. It's a foreign feeling for him, one which makes him even more afraid she will want to leave him.

Standing here watching her sit naked on that bed suddenly becomes torture because he just wants to touch her, and in this moment, he can't make himself.

Not until things are made even between them for his deception.

"You should get dressed," he says, picking up her clothing and carrying them over to place them on the bed in front of her. "We need to get back to our son."

"Isaac—"

"Now," he commands before swiping up his own shirt and sliding his arms in, then walking over to the door. "I shall await you outside the room."

He opens the door, walking out before he changes his mind and makes things even worse between them.

14

SIMONE

I'M NOT QUITE sure what the fuck just happened.

He went from the Master I know, to the man I'm in love with, to someone who won't even touch me like I know we both want him to, all within the short time we were in this room.

All which pisses me off and confuses me at the same time.

I get dressed though, knowing he's waiting for me outside, and when I'm done I take one more look around the room.

It's surreal, to see how much of this room I never got to explore, and knowing he used to be so close a lot of the time while I hadn't even known it.

Or had I?

Sometimes, I'd wake from a dead sleep thinking I heard a noise, but of course I'd never been able to see a thing.

Now…now I wonder if I felt his presence

nearby, if I'd known deep down inside that he was close and watching over me.

My eyes land back on the papers he tried to hand me, and finding a little trash can across the room, I pick them up off the bed and walk over to it.

It's clear he didn't understand why I don't want to see the papers. I could've told him why, but it felt pointless.

Why would I want to see proof of my ex-husband's deception? I don't want to know what he signed, what he had some woman sign as she forged my signature, and what things he said I would be okay with having done to me.

I lived it, and after my ex admitted it was all his doing, it's all I've ever needed to know.

As for what to do about Isaac's deception, I'm not sure.

Sure, I'm mad, but like he said, what could he possibly have said when he first approached me in the diner? How else should I have expected him to introduce himself to me knowing what little he knew?

He doesn't know how I feel about him, as Isaac or as my Master.

I don't even need to reconcile that they are both the same man, because my body and my heart knew, especially after the night he spent in my bed.

I'd been angry when I first realized it, but only

at myself. I should've seen it, I should've known, if for no other reason than the fact Malik resembles him a fair amount. And the way he likes the dark the most.

I'm not clueless though. I know why I haven't seen whats been staring me right in the face.

It's because of my pride. Since the moment he came into my life as Isaac, he's taken care of me in a way nobody else ever has. He wanted to make the situation right, and it was easier to believe a stranger wanted to help me than it was to think Master came after me, that he wanted me beyond this little room.

Now I know though, and I'm gonna do something about it.

With a final glance at the papers which started it all, I drop them into the trash can and turn on my heel, walking over and out the door, where the man I love is waiting for me on the other side.

As soon as we get up the steps, Isaac says he has work to do, kisses the top of my head, and disappears from my sight without another word. I head to the living room where we left Helen and Malik, but she isn't there, so I go upstairs to the bedroom.

When I enter, she turns from his crib and holds a finger up to her lips, walking away from it and toward me as quietly as she can. She takes my hand as she pulls me into the hallway, shuts the bedroom door, and leads us down the hall to one of the other rooms. Once there, she turns to me with a lifted brow, crossed arms, and eyes filled with concern.

"Out with it."

I want to tell her. Problem is, I haven't figured out what I should say to her. I'm not sure how she'll react. I know she loves me, but whether she's capable of understanding that what happened wasn't Isaac's fault is what holds me back from telling her the whole story.

"Helen, it's...complicated..."

Her face softens as she says gently, "Make no mistake, Simone. If I for one-second even thought that man was a bad one, I wouldn't have hesitated to say something quite loudly about it from the get go. You get me?" She sits down on the bed and pats the spot beside her as I nod, speaking again only once I've taken the seat as she's requested. "Now, wanna tell me how you didn't recognize the father of your child?"

Taking a deep breath, I start at the beginning, telling her everything that happened, and it's the first time I've talked about it out loud. All her emotions — from anger to worry to sadness — flit across her face as I talk, and by the end, I'm crying for the first time in a long while, as is she while holding me in her arms and hugging me tight.

"Your secret is safe with me, sweetie," she whispers as we separate, both of us swiping at our eyes. "You adore that man and he's done nothing but try to make things right for you and Malik. But I tell you what, he better be done with that business of his, because you're like a daughter to me since we met, and I'll kick his—"

"I am," Isaac's voice cuts in from out of nowhere, startling us both, and he chuckles as we both jerk our heads to look at where he stands in the doorway. "Done with 'that business' as you call it, that is. Therefore, no need for threats of violence, I assure you."

I'm the first to respond to his sudden appearance. "You are?"

Inclining his head, he slides his hands into his pockets, and levels his intense stare at me. "I was finished with the business long before you went home, Simone."

I want to ask why. I want it to be because he loves me, yet I'm afraid to know if it's not. So I change the topic while lowering my gaze, fearing he will see what I feel before I'm ready to tell him out loud. "You said you had work to do. It hasn't been long."

"I figured you and Helen would speak about everything after earlier. I have struggled with deciding how to tell you, let alone someone outside the situation, for a while now. I must admit I feared the worst when it came to how you would each react."

Even though I know he's done the best he could with this whole thing, I still want to make him pay for it a little. "Perhaps you should trust people a little more."

"It is difficult for me to trust anyone in normal circumstances, let alone one like ours where such actions would mess up the lives of a lot of people," he admits with a smile, walking closer to us before stopping to stand in front of where I sit on the bed. "But I am trying." He frowns a little, lifting a hand to swipe at my cheek with his thumb, where I'm sure the streaks from my tears are still visible. "After all, I am a private person, and it is not every day I let people get close to me, let alone bring them to live with me in my home."

I lift my brows in what I hope conveys surprise, trying to ignore the fact his hand is cupping my face, his thumb caressing my cheek in what one might consider a loving manner. "Oh? Is that what we're doing? Living here? And here I thought we were merely visiting."

"Simone—" Helen begins, stopping when Isaac holds up his free hand to stop her, his focus all on me.

"There are a lot of things I will tolerate," he says in an unbending tone, his eyes flashing with a heated warning. "You leaving my house with our son to live elsewhere is not one of them."

I like the possessiveness of his statement. It's clear in the way his jaw tightens imperceptibly, just like his hand on my face, and in his eyes. He may not be capable of declaring his feelings with words, but he is telling me what he feels in other ways. Something I know I must accept for now, because I get it; I get him.

And he gets me in a way nobody else ever has in my whole life.

"All right," I finally say, giving him a kind smile. "We won't."

"I know you will not."

He lowers his head, brushes his lips against mine, and then drops his hand as he steps back. His gaze sweeps me from head to toe, hot, fierce, and filled with promises for later.

Then, with a nod at Helen, he turns and exits the room without another word.

Leaving me happily anticipating the moment I'm alone with him as my Master again because there's no doubt in mind he plans to give us what we both need and want.

Finally.

15

SIMONE

THE NEXT EVENING, once Malik is asleep in his crib, Helen and I walk over to the door. As we reach it, she says, "Well, it's been an eventful and exhausting day. I'm gonna go to bed early if you don't mind."

"Of course I don't." Both of us step into the hallway and after she's shut the door softly behind us, I reach up and rest my hand on her upper arm, smiling as she looks at me. "Thanks for today. And every day. Not sure what I would've done without you all these months."

"It's not even worth thinking about truly. Everything is good now." She pats my hand, and I drop it as she steps away from me, glancing down the hall toward her room while yawning. "Night."

"Night."

I watch her until she disappears into her room before taking the few steps to mine, which isn't far from the room Isaac had made up for Malik, turning on the light as I enter and shut the door behind me.

I haven't seen Isaac since he disappeared last night, the only answer to any inquiry about where he is answered with "business" by Jim several times today, and recent experience shows chances are I will fall asleep before he climbs into bed with me. Thanks to that, I'm not even hopeful he'll fulfill the promise he made to me with his eyes roughly twenty-four hours ago. With that in mind, I let out a sigh heavy with disappointment, and head into the bathroom connected to my room.

Turning on the water after flipping the switch to keep the water in, I drizzle a little bubble bath into the stream, watching the bubbles quickly start to populate as I begin undressing. I run a brush through my hair while standing in front of the mirror once I'm naked, deciding it doesn't need washed before pinning it up and out of the way before climbing into the bathtub.

The heat of the water makes me gasp as it covers my body, and I turn the water off once it is high enough, before sitting back and letting my body adjust. With an arm on each side of the tub, I lean my head back and close my eyes, my body relaxing with the assistance of the jets once I've pushed the button that starts them. They are nearly silent, leaving me with nothing except my thoughts and the light whooshing sound of the water as company.

I'm not sure how much time passes, but the water's just beginning to cool when I hear my bedroom door close with what I'm sure is a deliberate amount of light force to warn me of Isaac's nearby presence. Even then, I'm slow to react, as if my time in the tub has put me in a trance; by the time I open my eyes and turn them toward the entryway, there he is. Leaning against the doorjamb with arms crossed, his eyes are filled with their usual blatant desire for me, and a naughty smile lights up his face as our gazes clash.

"This is a pleasant surprise," he says before straightening and walking closer, our eyes never leaving one another even as he sits on the edge of the tub. "Naked, warm, wet, and waiting for me. There is nothing else which makes me as happy as these things do."

"Truly?" I lift my brows in genuine surprise. "Nothing?"

"Well, perhaps a little less wet all over, as the only part of you which needs to be slick with arousal is that delectable pussy of yours." When he chuckles, I know it's because of the bright blush stealing over my cheeks at his words, which only deepens as he begins rolling up the sleeve covering his left arm. "I believe it is time for a little inspection, sweetheart."

His hand slips beneath the bubbles and into the water, his fingers gliding over my hip and across my stomach, until finally he reaches the juncture of my thighs. As he covers me with his palm, I bring my right leg up until it's bent at the knee, keeping my other mostly straight while spreading my legs as wide as they can go in this little space, and drop my head back against the tub's edge once more. He slips two fingers between the lips of my pussy, sliding them down and inserting them in a swift thrust that has me gasping, and flicks the pad of his thumb across my clit while curling the fingers now deep inside me. The action brings him into contact with my g-spot, and when he strokes it while pressing his thumb straight on my clit, my hips jerk up a bit in reaction, causing me to gasp in pure delight at the shockwaves of pleasure his expert touch brings.

And then, just as swiftly as he began touching me, his hand's gone and he towers over me as I continue to lounge in the tub.

"Stand up."

When he holds out a hand, I know exactly what he plans, and I'm all for it. I'm relieved, actually, because it's what we both want, and it's been too fucking long — well, barring the sleep sex that one day, which I don't count, and I've no doubt he doesn't include it either. I know exactly what I'll be getting, the thought alone making me lick my lips while I grab his hand, and he pulls me up at the same time his eyes drop to my mouth.

I step out, standing nude in front of him with my arms hanging at my sides, and he reaches for the towel hanging on the rack. I never knew the act of being dried off could be arousing, yet as he rubs me from top to bottom, the desire to jump his bones right here is nearly overpowering. Neither of us speak, with me lifting each arm when necessary, and then each foot as he bends down in front of me, only for him to glance up while down on his knees to stare right at the part of me which aches for him like nothing I've ever experienced before.

He drops the towel, causing me to squeak in surprise as he grabs my ass with both of his hands, leaning in to bury his face between my slightly parted legs while I grab onto his shoulders to anchor myself even though I know he won't let me fall. His deep intake of breath to take my scent in induces a dark flush which spreads from my face down the rest of my body, and when his tongue darts out to lick me as if he can wait no longer, only his strong grip keeps my legs from collapsing beneath me as my eyes slam shut.

Every inch of my body is electrified from his touch, so much I imagine if my skin could beg for his attention, it would without any hesitation. It responds to his touch like my heart responds to his voice — wholeheartedly.

But, as quick as his personal attention begins, it is over. He stands up and steps away after making sure I'm steady on my feet. Hanging up the towel, he walks to the door and grabs the robe, then strides back to me while holding it out with a broad smile. "Put this on so I may finish my inspection downstairs."

My mouth curves up in amusement at his statement as I take the robe from him, but he misses it because he turns away simultaneously, walking toward the door and opening it. By the time he looks back at me, I'm tying the robe's belt to keep it closed, stepping forward to take his hand with mine when he holds it out.

Without another word, his firm grips tugs me along behind him as he leads the way out of my room, down the steps, and in the direction of the door that leads to the basement. He continues holding my hand as he opens it, pulling me inside and down the illuminated walkway, and finally, down the long hallway to the room where he's going to finish what he started upstairs.

Only this time I know it's different from before, especially when he turns on the light inside before picking me up, and deposits me on the bed with a naughty grin.

And the transition...ah, I've never seen it prior to this moment, but I watch as he goes from Isaac to my Master — the man I love either way — right in front of where I rest in the center of the bed. His eyes flame, going from soft to glinting, while his frame straightens, and the air about him changes into one with even more authority and dominance than he already exudes on a regular basis.

"Don't move," he says as he starts at the top of his shirt, pushing the buttons through their holes one-by-one while staring at me as if he'll never get sick of doing so.

For a few seconds, the authority in his tone and the look on his face keeps me in place, drinking him in as he finishes unbuttoning his shirt and lets it fall to the ground. His chest muscles ripple, his arms dropping to his sides as he bunches his hands into fists, and when his eyes flash, I'm almost certain he's going to pounce me. Yet, he doesn't, his fists loosening once more while he lifts his hands to the belt of his buckle, and starts to remove it in a clear, leisurely fashion no doubt meant to torture both of us.

I stare, mesmerized, as he pulls the belt from the loops of his pants, all while recalling the way he'd used that belt on me the day he had to send me home. It's strange to see him half-naked — even that night in my bed I hadn't really looked at his practically naked form — yet exhilarating at the same time. He drops his arm straight down, the belt tip slapping against the floor, and I have to clench my thighs together at the desire pooling there as I admit to myself I wish he would hit me with it. Then I wonder if he's going to do exactly that as he steps close enough to the bed to touch the edge with his legs and smiles.

His command, when it comes, is soft and firm at the same time he lifts his hand and wraps the belt around his hand once, twice, all the while keeping his gaze locked on me. "On your knees."

The belt flashes out seconds later, making it clear I'm not moving fast enough to please him, and even though the tip barely licks the bottom of my bare foot, a flash of pain and trail of heat makes my nose tingle and eyes water.

"If you wish to play, *min elskede*, you must do as I bid immediately."

I blink at the foreign words, something I've never heard him include while speaking before, completely ignoring the warning in his words as I ask, "What did you just call me?"

With a flick of his wrist, he disregards my question, and sends the same lick of fire along the arch of my other foot, chuckling as I gasp and scramble to kneel on the bed in front of him.

He grins at me and says something foreign again, causing me to frown because he can't be saying what I think he's saying.

I raise my eyebrows while asking, "Go pee?"

"*God pige*," he repeats with a chuckle, lifting one hand to my face and cupping my cheek before translating. "Good girl."

Recalling the small amount of stuff I found about his background, I return his smile with one of my own. "You are speaking Danish?"

"*Ja*." He blinks and clears his throat as he

nods, clearly caught off guard, and states, "You researched me."

"Of course I did, although there wasn't a lot of information."

I only realize my words come across as accusatory when his eyes instantly shutter, the smile slipping away as he says, "Money can make anything disappear if one wishes it."

"Isaac—"

"*Nej.*" He cuts me off with a shake of his head, making it clear that what he just said means 'no,' the smile returning to his face while he visibly relaxes his shoulders after a few seconds. "I know you merely meant there is not much information about me, which is true, as well as it being my preference."

"You're different." Lifting a hand, I place it on his chest over his heart, our eyes nearly level with my kneeling position on the bed. "This is… nothing like before."

"As it should be, do you not agree? I am myself around you now, as I was not before, due to circumstances." With a tinge of amusement in his voice he remarks, "However, it has been a long time since my native language managed to slip through in my speech."

"I like it." Dropping my hand from his chest, I bring both of mine to the belt of the robe and start to untie it as I ask him, "What did the first thing you said mean?"

He smirks while taking a step back, dropping the belt to the floor with a clang, and crosses his arms over his chest as he watches me. "You will have to find out for yourself, hm?"

"I guess so." Finished, I open the robe and let it glide down my arms and off, where it falls to the bed and leaves me bared to Isaac's fierce, heated gaze.

My acquiescence doesn't last long as the teasing, playful part of me comes out to challenge the animal I know rests inside him. When he doesn't move toward me, I take the initiative, sliding off the edge of the bed and wedging myself between his body and it, before slowly lowering my form until I'm kneeling before him once more.

At the same time I lift my hands to the button of his pants, I lift my gaze to his in question, and he answers me by uncrossing his arms and placing them on the top of my head. As I lower my eyes and work to free him, he releases my hair from its restraints, causing it to fall down my back at the same time I finish unzipping him.

Using one hand on each side of his hips, I tug them down, the fact he's commando registering at the same time he steps out of his pants, and his hands drop to my shoulders with a single directive. "Up."

He's using his Master 'listen-to-me-or-else' tone then, but I ignore it while lifting a hand, wrapping my palm tight around the shaft of his cock and giving it a squeeze. His hands clench, digging into my shoulders, a soft 'fuck' escaping from his mouth as my tongue darts out to lick the tip a second before I wrap my lips around the head. Within seconds his hands spear into my hair, taking control of the situation, and holding my head in place as he begins fucking my mouth.

Closing my eyes, my body relaxes in the way he taught me, each of my hands moving to relax on his thighs to keep myself steady as I focus on pleasing him. I love the affinity between us and our mutual desire; how it's everything I remember and more, especially with us knowing each other more intimately now.

I take great pleasure from the possessive hold he has on me. Physically, mentally, and emotionally, there's no question I am his in every single way, and we both know it. After all this time, and everything I've been through, it's still hard to imagine myself as truly Isaac's, no — as my *Master's* — something I dreamt about every single waking moment we were apart.

When he thrusts hard deep into my throat, I take him all the way in with the ease of familiarity and practice, his groan erupting at the same time I moan. My whole body reacts to the manner in which he's treating me, like his slut and his beloved one at the same time, present in his primal fucking of my mouth even as his grip on my head is gentle yet firm. I'm so turned on, my arousal wets my thighs, my pussy begging for the attention he's currently bestowing me orally.

He pauses in his movements out of nowhere, pulling out slowly as he murmurs, "You will stand up without speaking, walk over to the center beam, and stand there facing toward the wall with your feet spread slightly, your hands clasped and held up straight in the air."

Releasing his hold on me, he steps back as I rise and rush to do as he's directed because I'm eager to please him. Moving into position, I do my best to hold it while listening to him move around the room since I can't see him.

And even though I'm not supposed to speak, the moment I feel him standing behind me as he binds my hands with the hanging ties above my head to keep them exactly where he wants, I ask with an excited grin, "Does this mean you're finally going to fuck me with the lights on?"

16

ISAAC

SHE'S A MASTERPIECE...AND she's all his.

That's the first thing Isaac thinks as he walks around to stand in front of Simone, her disobedient question hanging in the air between them. He should punish her for speaking after he commanded her not to, but all is forgiven for *that* transgression at the ravishing smile on her face.

And frankly he can't wait to fuck her with the lights on.

So, instead of responding to her question, he lifts a brow and simply says, "I believe there is a punishment to dole out, is there not?"

He loves the instant reaction his words elicit from her. With her flushed complexion, dilated pupils, and soft parted lips, she's a beautiful vision he never wants deprived of ever again. Lifting a hand to her face, he cups her cheek, and the moment his thumb strokes gently across her chin, she automatically straightens her back and moves into his touch as taught.

Without even thinking about it, he returns to the role he plays best; the part they both enjoy tremendously.

His next words are controlled and in charge as they stare intently at one another. "Pick your implement, *min elskede*."

Smiling, she makes it obvious she remembers this game, her eyelids drifting shut nice and slow before they rise again, hunger for him clear in her gaze. "Your hand."

The vision of her delightful skin turning red and flushed from the smack of his hand against it has him itching to begin, a feeling he has no reason to ignore. However, there's one thing he needs from her first.

"Before we begin," he says as his hand moves, skimming down from her face until it encircles her throat, resting there with a slight pressure to keep her still. "Do we not both have roles when in this room? What is yours, hm?"

"I'm whatever you desire me to be."

"Good girl." He steps closer, his hand tightening enough to elicit a tiny gasp from her, and making her eyes go round in surprise as well as delight with their bodies nearly touching everywhere. "And mine?"

He loves the breath-taking grin she gives him in spite of her current position, all the feelings he is sure she doesn't want him to know about shining bright from her eyes. Feelings he hasn't felt in a long time himself and ones he is not ready to share with her yet, which mean he cannot ask her to share her own.

But when he does, he imagines it will be everything he has always desired from the moment he had first lain his hands upon her.

"Master," she finally whispers. "My Master."

"Are you certain?"

Her voice remains soft and steady along with her trust-filled gaze. "Yes, Master."

"And your name?" His free hand comes up to rest at her waist, the hand on her throat sliding down her body until it's on the other side of her waist, and he moves into her until every inch of her is in contact with him. "What is your name?"

She responds with the answer he taught her the first time. "I'm called only what you wish to call me, Master."

"I am pleased you remember." He pauses for effect, his fingers on her waist gripping her, making it clear she's his at the same time he lowers his face until their lips are only a breath apart. "Once I say your name, you are mine. There is no backing out. I will never let you go."

"I became yours the moment you claimed me, Master."

"Correct. You belong to me and only me. In every aspect of our life together, you will treat me as your Master. In the polite company of others, you will not kneel, but stand by my side and support me in whatever capacity I need or want. However, this privilege has its perks. You will maintain your position as lady of the household and the mother of Malik, as well as our future children. And no matter what, you are free to inform me at any time whether something will interfere with your caring of the children, because we cannot have you indisposed. Therefore, if something will impair your ability to care for them — beyond those of which I am already aware — you must tell me immediately. Do you understand?"

He loves the way her eyes seem to melt at what he's just said, and she nods at the same time she replies, "Yes, Master, I understand."

"Excellent. When we are not in this room, you will use my given name, although a term of endearment is desirable as well. In this room, I am and will remain Master. As for you," he murmurs, grinding his stiff arousal against her suggestively before pressing a soft kiss against her mouth. "You will remain Simone, in and out of this room, because it is your name, which belongs to you and nobody else. However, terms of endearments are my preferred way of addressing you, and shall most likely remain so."

Confusion clouds her eyes, perhaps because of his calling her Cara the other day, and realizes he must clarify why the change; something he does quite happily as he keeps her as close to him as two humans can possibly get without being intimate.

"The first time you were here, you were not truly mine. As my job, I renamed the slaves because it allowed us to bond in a way necessary for that type of relationship, but without giving our true selves to someone who was not our real partner."

He watches her eyes lighten, some of the confusion clearing as her eyes drop to his mouth, and it takes every ounce of his control not to pounce her because of it. "Many use the renaming progress to make someone their own, to break them down into what they want that person to be, but I have never used it as such as I have no right to turn someone into something they are not…especially when the experience was something they paid for."

And you didn't, is the thought left unfinished.

But she doesn't miss a thing, her fiery eyes snapping back up to his even as she continues to speak in a gentle understanding tone. "You can't continue to blame yourself; I won't have it."

"Indeed?" His tone is sharp, but his underlying amusement is evident in the slight curve of his lips. "I did the very thing I did not desire to do to anyone, let alone you, because we both had no idea, but it was my business. My job was to know exactly what went on at any time, yet you were broken down and built up again due to my failure."

He lifts his index finger to her lips to keep her from speaking any further as he shakes his head. "True, I cannot undo it, and you are here with me anyway, but I do not deny the truth. Such a thing is dangerous, and with that, you will remain Simone since that is your true identity. In the context of our connection, and our past together, I must return it to you."

The burning irritation in her gaze changes to unmistakable passion, her lips curving up beneath the touch of his finger seconds before her tongue darts out and she licks him, giggling. "I accept the return of my name, Master, and thank you, but as always, I am whatever you wish to call me."

"As if you have any other option in this matter."

"Actually, I do." When he growls low in his throat at her impertinence, she laughs and licks his finger again. "But I don't want one. I'm not upset. I don't blame you, I could've walked away when I first knew, and I didn't. I'm here of my own free will, I'm happy, and I'm yours. I don't want to talk about it anymore, so how about you just stop teasing us both and put me to good use."

He doesn't doubt her sincerity in the slightest, and he knows it's because she has feelings for him, but a tiny part of him can't shake the notion she thinks this way because of her time spent as his slave. There is no way to make sure though, and right now, they both want the same thing.

Stepping back, there's no warning from him to her before he lifts his right hand high, and in one swift motion brings it down to slap her left breast. Her body jerks, a gasp of pleasure followed by a moan escaping her luscious mouth at the same time her eyes drift shut.

The sight gives him a whole new perspective on her reactions from the first moment she'd spent in this room. With one slap, her cheeks are a rosy blush on her high cheekbones, her lips slightly open and wet from her licking them, and she wore an indisputable expression showcasing her pleasure mixed with pain. The long-term ache in his chest, the one he'd had since learning the truth about everything, lessoned in its intensity at the realization she truly was enjoying herself, and not just saying so for his preference.

"You will count," he directs her, raising his hand once more. "For that mouth of yours since the moment of your arrival, until it pleases me to stop. Starting with the one you just received, now."

Her response is instant, strong, and loaded with joy as her eyes remain shut. "One."

Hitting her again on the other breast, the bloom of pink on her skin in the shape of his handprint, and her calling out "Two!" in a breathy, pleasure packed verbalization keeps his cock hard and aching to get inside her. After delivering hits three and four, both of which she counts without missing a beat, he steps close once more and grabs her by the hips.

"Turn and face the beam."

The ties keep her from getting away, but her feet remain on the ground, leaving her far away enough from the beam she won't hit it along with allowing him to walk around her if he wants to. Not necessary, of course, since her turning around gives him a full-lighted view of her backside, the perfect location for the rest of her discipline before the real enjoyment of each other begins.

Dropping his hands from her body once again, he walks over to where his belt is and picks it up, placing the buckle in his right palm before wrapping the belt around it, leaving half of it dangling from his grasp while standing behind her in a position that will allow him to achieve his desired results. Next to seeing her face while they fuck for the first time, this is also the first time he gets to see the results of his handiwork for more than just a few minutes.

"Master?" She doesn't do anything other than whisper the word, keeping her head forward and her body still, but it's enough to knock him out of his thoughts.

He flicks his wrist, the belt snapping just enough for the tip to contact her left ass cheek, and her yelp of surprise quickly turns into a moan as she wiggles her ass. Yes, she'd said she wanted his hand, but the belt mixed with his towering height will work better at this time and angle. Plus, her reaction tells him it doesn't matter at this point; she's enjoying every second of it.

"Forgetting something?" He asks, tapping the belt against his leg as he waits for her reply, which comes an instant later as she goes still once more.

"Five."

The belt is firm and controlled in his grip as he elevates his arm, keeping the swing light as he brings it forward and lands perfectly, her skin rising pink where the strike landed.

Her reaction is only a hiss this time as her body jerks and her hands tighten around the ties above her head as she says, "Six."

The next three come in rapid succession, her body relaxing and swaying even as her grip tightens, her utterances of the count lost in her vocal reactions to the smacks against her body.

On the tenth one, she cries out the number and the belt slips from his grip to the ground as he steps forward to release her, her body going limp. With one arm around her waist, he undoes the ties, and turns her until she faces him.

Face flushed and damp, she lifts her passionate gaze to his, smiles wide, and wraps her arms around his neck. When her mouth opens a little as they stare at one another, he can tell she wants to say something, so he nods. "You may speak freely."

She blinks, swallowing audibly, her gaze skittering away before returning just as quick to his, her smile turning shy as she whispers, "I missed that. You…you've made me feel a way I never could've imagined, let alone knew I could want."

When her eyes start to water, he opens his mouth to speak, but she shakes her head and opens up to him in a way he hadn't thought would happen so soon. "I was heartbroken when you took me home that day. I didn't intend to tell you this; I wanted to make you pay for keeping the truth from me, but I can't. I never feared you, not for a second, and you took care of me. You made me feel safe, even when you did things to me I never thought I would like."

A tear slips down her cheek when she finishes with, "I love you. As Isaac. As my Master. And I don't want you to say it back to me, not right now. And I mean that, it's not a ploy. I want you to say it when you mean it and not just because I have—"

Isaac leans in and captures her lips with a punishing kiss, trying to staunch the flow of words from her lips, every single one stabbing his heart due to her earnest delivery. He can't take it, not right now, not when he's not completely sure he deserves her complete devotion in any way.

This woman, the one he's come to care about more than he ever planned to care for another, is strong; stronger than even him, because even after being betrayed she hadn't cut her heart off. She loves him and wants him anyway, and for him, that's a strange concept to wrap his head around.

Someone hurt him once, and he vowed nobody would ever get that close to him again, but meeting her had changed it all and he wasn't sure what to do with it now that it's crystal clear where she stands, although he certainly thought so from nearly the moment they'd met again.

So he does as she requests — even though he had no intention of telling her his feelings when he isn't even sure of them himself anyway — and says nothing as he slips a hand up and into her hair, holding her head still with his firm grip. Her lips part underneath his without any prompting, and when his tongue invades her mouth, she moans as if it's the best kiss they've ever had. As if revealing her feelings has somehow changed the way everything feels.

The fanciful thought makes him pull away from her, keeping the hand in her hair as he steps to the side and tugs her forward, saying in more of a forceful voice than he intends, "Center of the bed on your back, legs spread with your hands above your head."

She doesn't argue when he lets go of her hair, staying silent while walking toward the bed and climbing on, only to look over her shoulder with a smirk as she slowly crawls into place to deliberately tease him. Once she's in the center, she turns onto her back, bends both her legs with her feet flat on the bed, and spreads both wide just as he told her too. Then, with a sigh, she lifts her hands above her head, resting them on the pillow beneath her head.

His eyes travel from her hands down to her face where she has her eyes closed and lips parted, her breathing deep and even. His gaze continues its perusal of her lush form down to her breasts, her nipples tight and begging for his touch, and keeps going until his sight lands on her pussy, clean shaven and glistening with the evidence of her arousal.

She's always been ready for him. He barely had to touch her to get her going once things had begun, and apparently that hasn't changed, which only makes his decision in this moment as easy as he's hoped it would be. Stalking toward the bed, he's looking forward to the one thing they've yet to do: they'll fuck with the lights on, with her lying on her back just like that, so he can witness the pleasure he knows will be written all over her face.

He's going to relish every moment of it.

And with that thought, he's on his knees, with her spread out before him and one leg on each side of where he's kneeling. The first touch of his hand on her pussy is rough with impatience. Moaning, she moves into his caress, the motion causing his index finger to slip between her labia, before sliding it deep inside her. She arches her back, especially when he inserts a second finger, curling both to caress her g-spot until she starts to squirm in her desperation to get off.

Unwilling to wait any longer, Isaac repositions his body so it's covering her, staring down at her glowing face and lust-filled gaze with his own, his cock poised at her entrance and ready for the moment they've both been waiting for. Her legs come up to wrap around his waist of their own volition, her arms stealing around his neck as she smiles giddily at him.

Her hips lift at the same time he surges forward, seating himself deep inside her with a loud groan of satisfaction as her pussy clenches every inch of him. Her arms tighten about his neck as she gasps and closes her eyes, her body stiffening in a way that makes it evident she needs a moment to adjust to his size once again.

Remembering the first time he'd ever fucked her, he does the same as before and remains still so she may adjust to his size, and he's pleased when not even a minute later, she's moving her hips up and toward where they're connected. Amused at the small whimpers of pleasure falling from her lips, he holds completely still as she uses what little maneuverability she has to fuck him, watching the maelstrom of emotions — mostly pleasurable — flit over her face.

And as her movements become more frenzied, she clings to him in every possible way. When her pussy clamps down on his cock, it jerks him from where he's focused on her expressive face, his next words coming out with more force than he intends. "You will not come without my permission, Simone."

Pressing his body down on hers so she's trapped against the mattress, her eyes pop open and she glares at him, her mouth turning down in an adorable pout. "Please," she whispers, trying to move her hips once more and finding it impossible to do anything with his weight upon her as it is. "Please, Master. I was almost there. Let me come, please."

He doesn't reply, mostly because the way she asks isn't what he wants to hear from her. So, he captures her lips with his, conquering her mouth at the same time he pulls out and plunges back in.

Over and over, fast and hard strokes that go so deep inside her, it distracts her from kissing him back, and he chuckles as she simply pants and whimpers into his mouth at the pleasure. Her arms move until she's gripping his shoulders, her nails digging into the skin as she tries to stave off her body's natural response, her whimpers turning into moans as her whole body quivers with her efforts.

Knowing she can take it, he drives into her repeatedly, drawing them both closer to the edge until she's shaking and sobbing, ripping her mouth away to cry out, "Please, M-master, may I come for you?"

"Yes." He maintains his pace as he answers her, knowing she's going to shatter around him, and he'll be joining her. "Come for me like the good slut you are, Simone. Come now."

His words are all she needs, her whole body tensing up as her nails break the skin on his shoulders, and she tosses her head back to scream from the force of her orgasm. He slides his cock in and out a few more times, her body relaxing as he thrusts hard one final time and finishes inside her with a deep, satisfied groan into her neck.

Then, when the intimacy of this position allows her to turn her head and kiss his cheek as they both lie there recovering, Isaac knows one thing for certain — there isn't a chance in hell he'll ever let Simone go if he can help it, because she is definitely the perfect woman for him.

Which means he better make sure he's the man she deserves because she warrants nothing less than his all.

17

SIMONE

Life with Isaac turns into something quite interesting after the night we finally have sex again.

In some ways, many things stay the same for the next two weeks. He spends lots of time with me, Malik, and Helen when he isn't working on one thing or another.

Earlier today I learned his 'Master/slave' business had been only one of many dealings he was involved in. However, most of them are hobbies, and he actually finances a lot of people's ventures who can't obtain traditional funding. Not in a shady way though; more like someone thinking the business isn't viable for one reason or another. When I asked Isaac why he would take the risk — because it's obvious there is a big chance he'll lose his money — he told me there isn't much in life without risk, and he's got more than enough money that losing some of it trying to help people realize their dreams is a small price to pay.

I fear his non-concern about spending money is something I'll never be able to understand after what I've been through, but what's even better is how he is slowly letting his true self shine through more and more every day.

Like right now.

Standing in the doorway to Malik's room, Isaac sits in a chair with his son in his lap, reading a book to him. The funny part is, he'll read the sentence in English as it's printed, and then say it again, except this time it's in Danish. And every single time he does that, Malik's little head lifts to stare at his father with an adorably confused expression.

A little over six months old now, he's grown so much in the time we've been here, and although he can be a bit wobbly, he's able to sit up on his own. I'll often catch Isaac walking with him around the room, Malik's fingers wrapped around each of his, and every time that moment makes it clear I've made the right choice.

Not that I ever seriously considered doing anything else once I found out who he was, even if it had angered me. I'm not mad anymore for sure, and even if he doesn't love me, I know he cares for me and that's more than I've ever had my whole life with anyone else besides Helen.

And speaking of her, I'm pretty positive she's

got a thing for Jim. Even though she still refers to him as "The Undertaker," it's gone from a look of annoyance to one with a soft smile and a sideways glance every time he's in the room. I'm not sure they've done anything together, but I think even if I asked her, she wouldn't tell me anyway, although they are certainly closer in age to one another than me and Isaac are.

Just as I'm about to step back with that thought so Isaac can have more alone time with Malik, he looks up after kissing the top of our son's head and spots me.

"Se, Malik, det er din mor," he says while looking straight at me, making a face when he realizes he's not speaking English again and corrects himself. "I told him 'Look, Malik, it is your mommy.' I do not believe he finds the language as interesting as I think he should."

"Ah," I reply with a soft laugh as I walk in and across the room to where they're sitting. "Even if that's the case, which it isn't, he will be speaking both languages before you know it. He's listening even if he can't repeat what you've said."

"Perhaps."

"You don't know much about children at all, do you?" As he shakes his head, I stop beside the chair and take a seat on the arm of it, where automatically slides his now free hand around my waist to keep me there. "Well, you seem like a fast learner. And it's a fact that he picks up on the language, and therefore words with their meanings, all around him."

Malik squeals, smiling at me as he finally realizes I'm close by. A second later he starts gnawing on the corner of the board book, the drool from his efforts dripping onto Isaac's hand, to which he responds with an amused mutter that makes me laugh again. "Yuck."

"I think he's teething. He's been trying to chew on everything."

"He is," comes Helen's soft response from the doorway, stepping inside as we both look toward her. "I saw two little white teeth starting to make their appearance earlier today. And," she continues with a pointed look at Isaac, "I've been sent to tell you you've got a business associate waiting for you in your office."

Isaac lifts his drool-covered hand, cursing as he looks at his watch before letting go of my waist, and picks up his son with both hands while rising from the chair. Then Isaac gives the top of his head a kiss and holds him out to me, giving me a peck on the cheek once I'm holding our son in my arms. Stepping back, he wipes his hand on his pants as he speaks.

"Try to stay awake until I join you this evening. I need to speak with you about something important."

A nod while wondering what he wishes to speak with me about is all I'm able to muster as he stares at me for another few moments before turning on his heel and heading out of the room.

Helen walks toward me, taking Malik from my arms once she's close as he starts flailing his arms at the sight of her, gurgling with happiness. After giving him an exaggerated and loud kiss on his cheek, which makes me laugh even harder, her eyes practically twinkle as she says, "That man is so in love with you. But I imagine he hasn't told you."

"He hasn't." Shrugging, I drop down to sit in the chair and sigh. "I don't think he knows what he feels, honestly. I mean, it's obvious he cares for me, nobody can deny that. But love? I don't think he knows what that is."

"Sure he does," she assures me in a gentle tone. "If you ask me, he's been hurt by someone; perhaps that woman he was engaged to in the past?"

With another lift of my shoulders, I say, "Dunno. He doesn't talk about it all that much, and I think he likes it that way. He knows how I feel about him; if he wants to share, I'm sure he will in his own time."

"He does seem to want everything his way, that's true."

Smirking at that precise statement, a long drawn-out yawn escapes from me at the same time Malik starts fussing in Helen's embrace. She shakes her head when I stand up to take him, rocking him in her arms while tilting her head toward the door.

"Go get a relaxing bath and maybe a little nap so you're still awake later like he asked. I'll get Malik ready for bed and put him down for the night."

"Are you sure?" I know she is, but I ask anyway. I love spending time with Malik and her, and sometimes I feel like she puts him down to bed more than I do, yet that's not true. This is the first time in a week, mostly because I've wanted her to feel like the friend she is, rather than a caretaker. When she lifts a brow and purses her lips, I lift my hands up in surrender and say, "Okay, okay, I'm going. Thank you, as always, and I'll see you in the morning."

After a final nod and smile from Helen, I kiss Malik goodnight, and head back to my bedroom to do exactly as Helen suggested.

Starting a hot bath, I walk over to the sink to brush out my hair in preparation for washing it, and can't help but admire my body once I've taken all my clothes off. I'm marked all over my chest from Isaac's mouth, especially his teeth, and the sight of it has the effect of turning me on. It's great, and terrifying all at once, because all I have to do is think about him putting his hands on me in whatever fashion he likes, and desire sparks to life in an instant.

Sighing heavily and picking up the hairbrush,

I pull it through my hair while wondering what kind of business Isaac is dealing with, and how long it will take. Mostly because I want to know what he wishes to discuss with me.

When it comes to sex, he's still my Master, but outside it…it's almost like we're married. At least, he treats me that way, but I'm not sure he'll ever ask me to marry him. I know about his broken engagement and he hasn't even spoken about it with me, so to me, that indicates he's not ready to marry anyone else either. And in all honesty, I'm not sure I want to get married again either; the first time hadn't turned out good at all.

On the other hand, Isaac and my ex-husband are too totally different men, and even if I am not certain what Isaac feels for me, I am completely confident he would never do to me what Henry had.

Ugh, I hate feeling one way while wanting another thing with everything in me.

Who am I kidding? I would love nothing more than to marry Isaac and have more children with him, especially after seeing him with Malik. The man, in my eyes, was made to have children of his own; the love for his son can't be missed for sure. I'm blessed it worked out that way, because it sure as hell could've been worse, and I know it.

Finished with brushing out my hair, I walk over to the tub and climb in, hissing a little as the hot water covers me while I lower my body into it.

Once I'm adjusted, I lean my head back and simply enjoy the water swishing for a little while, only starting to wash my hair and such when the water starts to cool.

After climbing out, drying off, and getting dressed, I head to bed for a little nap, knowing even if I'm not awake when Isaac comes to bed, he will wake me up as he always does.

Only when I finally open up my eyes, it's the next morning...with both Isaac and Jim nowhere to be found, and nobody able to tell me where they went.

18

ISAAC

Isaac's phone dings as he sits in his office minutes after his business associate leaves, a meeting which had honestly taken longer than he'd expected it to. A lot longer, which is why he'd sent Jim a few minutes ago to check and see if Simone has fallen asleep already.

With a frustrated sigh, he lifts his phone off of the desk to see who is texting him this late, only to stop cold at the message staring at him from the tiny box on the screen.

"She's missing. You need to come now."

"Fuck." Standing up, he looks at the time, only to realize it's ten after midnight, and grabs his jacket before exiting the room with a bellowed, "Jim!"

Of course, Jim appears almost instantly from out of nowhere, and even after all these years, Isaac isn't sure how the man manages it. However, he's hardly going to question the man he's not sure he could do without now about something such as that.

"Sir?"

"We have to leave right now. Lizzy is missing; I just received a message from her father, the fucking fool."

His horrified expression matches how Isaac feels, because both know what this means, and he nods. "I will get the car and call security, sir." He catches Isaac looking toward the part of the house where Simone, Malik, and Helen are, and says in a hushed voice, "They are in bed already and sleeping. If we leave now, we will most likely return before they even awake in the morning, sir."

"And if we are not?"

"Wait and see, sir. If it looks as if it will take longer, you may message her, but if you do it now, you will wake her. Do you really wish to waste time now in order to answer the questions she will have?"

Isaac knows Jim is right, even if he doesn't want to leave them here with no explanation, and what Simone will no doubt find as a scary looking security guard. Something tells him he will regret not waking her up and informing her, but there is truly no time to waste.

With marked reluctance, he says, "Lets go then."

It's about a half hour drive, during which

Isaac worries more about Simone waking up to find him not there than the current situation, but upon arrival they are let in with ease.

The last thing Isaac wants is to be here. If he could have nothing to do with Lizzy or her life any longer, he would feel nothing except relief. This bullshit has been going on too long, but trying to convince her father of that is another matter. The man is more stubborn and protective than Isaac, yet Isaac wouldn't be so stupid as to fail to recognize when someone is harming those around them more than anything else.

"Winston," Isaac says, greeting the butler as the door opens.

"Mister Toft," he responds with an incline of his head as he steps back, letting Isaac and Jim step inside before shutting the door behind them. "Mister Parker awaits you in his office. Follow me."

Isaac waves him off with his hand before shrugging out of his jacket. "I know the way, thank you."

"Absolutely."

Winston disappears, and Isaac hands Jim his jacket along with instructions. "You know what to do. Go ask questions, see if anybody knows where she might have run off to, if she has been talking about anyone she might persuade to help her, etcetera."

"On it, Sir."

Jim heads one way after hanging up the jacket, and Isaac walks down the long hallway before making a left, and stepping inside the room, his presence immediately noticed by the man who was to have been his father-in-law.

The same man who lied about his daughter's sickness in hopes somebody would marry and take care of her.

A man with a daughter who tried to kill Isaac a few weeks before their wedding, and had only escaped going to prison or mental institution because Isaac refused to have his private life become a public spectacle.

"Isaac," Alfred Parker acknowledges him with a tight smile while nodding toward the chair in front of the desk. "Have a seat."

"Alfred," he responds while walking inside and shutting the door behind him. "I would rather stand, as you know."

Grimacing, Alfred stands up and walks over to the bar, pouring himself some Scotch before proffering the bottle at Isaac with a lift of his brow. "Drink?"

"I am not here for social chit chat." He tries to keep the exasperation out of his voice so Alfred won't get defensive and keep this meeting going forever with his attitude. "Where has your daughter run off to now?"

"Hell if I know," he mutters, taking a huge gulp of his drink, and looking over at Isaac with pain-filled eyes. "We tried to find her before involving you, but she's been gone over twenty-four hours now. We've no idea where to look."

"She is supposed to be under watch at all times, Alfred. That was the deal. How the hell did she escape?"

"Seduced the guard, I suspect, since he's missing as well."

"Terrific."

"You'll find her won't you?"

"Do I have a fucking choice?" Isaac runs a hand through his hair in frustration, stalking over to the window and taking a deep breath before turning around to glare at Alfred. "Do us all a favor: get female guards next time and do not allow them to ever be alone with her. I hope she has not harmed anyone by the time we find her, although at least she would be locked up if she did."

"She wouldn't be able to handle it, Isaac, and you know it."

"Who gives a shit, besides you? Yes, she is your daughter, but you cannot allow her to mess with the lives of others because you wish to keep your precious daughter with you. She is *sick*, and she always will be. You need to learn to accept it!"

The fact Alfred starts crying has Isaac making a sound of disgust and walking over to the door. He turns back to Alfred who pours himself another drink and says, "I will find her. And if she has managed not to get herself in trouble, we will be discussing other options. I am fed up with picking up your slack, Alfred, especially for a woman I want nothing more than to never lay eyes upon ever again."

"I'm sorry, Isaac——"

"You are always sorry, Alfred." Isaac knows he's letting his anger get the best of him, but at this point, perhaps showing a little anger is a necessity to get through to this man. "Now is the time to stop apologizing and start doing something about it. I will return with your daughter, and I hope for your sake she is simply out having fun and not causing havoc."

And with those final words, he goes to look for Jim so they can locate Lizzy before she does something stupid or dangerous.

Or both.

"Sir."

Isaac rouses from his nap at the small press of Jim's hand against his shoulder, sitting up straight and running a hand through his hair as Jim reclaims his seat across the center. They were parked at the last place they checked, both of them needing to rest a bit before continuing — especially Jim since he drove — but he must've slept a little longer than he intended.

Lifting his arm to check his watch, Isaac curses at seeing it is ten o'clock, and reaches into his pocket for his cell phone while addressing Jim. "She hasn't called?"

"I called the house at nine, sir. At the time, security informed me they headed out to go shopping at the mall nearly an hour earlier."

Amused, he lifts a brow at Jim, and then glares down at his phone. "And she didn't even bother to call me?"

"Security informed her you were called away on urgent business late last night right after your meeting and would be back as soon as possible. Apparently she hadn't even been angry; just announced she wished to go out to the store."

"She is a strange creature," he mutters, only to jerk his head up at the sound of Jim chuckling. "What, exactly, is humorous?"

"That she is, sir. Same as you. Also, I assume she is rather secure with your relationship, which isn't surprising; she did declare her love for you, after all."

Isaac takes Jim's words to heart because he knows they are true. He should be nothing more than pleased that Simone feels the way she does, and deems him a person she may trust implicitly, enough to not even question him leaving late at night on business. The problem is, he still is not sure he deserves such devotion and blind faith from her, although that is not going to stop him from making her his in every way imaginable.

And speaking of, the fact this little search derailed his plans for Simone and himself last evening really pisses him off, because he and Jim have yet to even gain a hint of where Lizzy has gone. She appears to have vanished into thin air, although he is sure that is the doing of the man she apparently ran off with.

If he weren't already intimately acquainted with her crazy tendencies, he would just say fuck it, fuck her, and leave her to whatever the hell she is doing with her life. Because all he wishes to do is return home to his son and the woman he hopes will be his wife sooner rather than later.

He has no doubt he would've been an engaged man by now if it weren't for the overlong meeting with his business associate and then this problem with Lizzy cropping up. At his request, Jim had set up a table for two in the playroom, with a whole dinner planned for the both of them, where he'd planned to propose to Simone.

Frustrated and pissed, he dials Alfred, hoping Lizzy has contacted her father, so he can go home and figure out a way to make sure this toxic woman and her father are out of his life once and for all.

The moment Alfred answers the phone, Isaac snaps, "Have you heard from her?"

"No." Alfred sounds tired, perhaps even

broken down, but Isaac can't even summon the smallest sympathy for this man who almost succeeded in tricking him into marrying his psychopath of a daughter.

Okay, that description is not completely accurate, but the woman had tried to kill him after all.

"Any — *any* — fucking idea where she might be at all? She could not have gone far. What did this guy even look like, the one you believe she ran off with?"

"I—I can't say for sure. He was nondescript. Not too big, not too small. Plain." Alfred growls in frustration. "Fuck! It didn't matter, son, he was simply supposed to guard her."

His skin crawls at the use of that word from Alfred's mouth. "I am not, nor will I ever be, your son. And how the hell do you not know what the man guarding your daughter looked like? Do you even know his name?"

"Uh…no. I didn't hire him and never saw him personally; I had the other security staff do it. He hadn't been here long, maybe a week or two."

He pinches the bridge of his nose, anger surging through him at this man's incompetence. "For fuck's sake. I would ask how the hell you raised a child to adulthood, but it is apparent you probably did not have much to do with that either." Then, shoving a hand through his hair, Isaac smirks at the sight of Jim attempting to hide his amusement, and takes a deep breath before continuing. "I will give it another hour or two; after that, I am calling the police Alfred. I am done with you and—"

"Isaac. Please. I did the best I could. I didn't know she would hurt you, she's always been in love with you—"

Cutting him off, Isaac practically growls into the phone. "No. She did not fucking love me, she was obsessed with me Alfred. There is a difference, and I almost paid for it with my fucking life. Prepare to be questioned by the police if I am unable to locate her soon."

Pressing the end button on a phone call has never felt so satisfying as it does in this moment. Only his relief doesn't last long as Jim's phone rings, both their eyebrows rising at the sight of Helen's name on the screen, and Jim answers it with a forced calm in his voice.

"Hello?"

Isaac is able to hear her practically screaming something, yet isn't able to make out her exact words.

When Jim's eyes round, his face paling as it fills with dread, he stares at Isaac while continuing to speak into the phone. "Are you certain?" More rushed words from her, followed by Jim closing his eyes and gulping, and Isaac's stomach tightens with dread. "Oh, god. Don't move and try to stay calm. We'll be there as soon as we can get there."

"What the fuck—"

"Sir," Jim cuts Isaac off as he moves to sit next to him while closing his phone, his hand shaking as he grips it. "Helen says she went to the bathroom, leaving Simone and Malik looking at children's clothes, and when she came back not even five minutes later, they were gone. She said she's been looking for a half hour, but they're nowhere to be found—"

His sentence is left unfinished as his phone buzzes, sending his anger and increasing dread through every inch of him at the sight of Lizzy's name on his screen, and he opens it to read whatever she's sent him.

"Looking for me? I'm glad. After all, I've been waiting to see you for so long."

Not even bothering to text her back, he hits the button to call her, only for it to go straight to voicemail. Irate, he starts to text her back, but is stopped as a new message arrives.

"I don't want to talk on the phone. I need to see you. You know you want to see me."

"I don't," he responds with banked rage. *"I'm sick of these games, Lizzy. You need to go home, now, and I've come to take you. Where are you?"*

He knows it is stupid to say that. She planned this, she knew he would come after her; after all, this is not the first fucking time she has done this, but if he has anything to do about it, it will for sure be the fucking last time.

"Come here. I've got something to show you." She gives the address of a hotel not even five minutes away from where they sit downtown. *"Trust me. You don't want to miss this."*

The apprehension he felt at hearing Simone and Malik went missing in the mall builds to terror at the thoughts swarming in his head. Is Lizzy responsible for it all? Had she planned this? How? How had she even known? Her father? The guard? If he had any enemies, he wasn't aware of them, but it is entirely plausible that he pissed someone off in the past, especially during his relationship with Lizzy.

Fuck, if she had something to do with this and Simone or Malik gets hurt, he'll never forgive himself for not doing what should've been done when she tried to kill him.

"Sir?"

Gritting his teeth, he looks up and addresses a highly concerned Jim, rattling off the address to the hotel. "Stop here on the way. Lizzy is claiming she has something I need to see. I am afraid she has gone off the deep end, and may indeed be the reason Simone and Malik are missing."

"Are you coming? Don't you want to see what I have for you? Don't you want to be a family? :) Come alone."

God, she's really lost it this time.

"Shall I call the police, sir?" Jim asks, once again catching Isaac's attention, opening the door in order to exit. "Time may be of the essence."

"No. We shall go there first. It is likely she and this idiot of a guard, who may be as sick as she, did this to get my attention and they are with her."

Nodding, Jim looks as terrified at that as Isaac feels, and after stepping out shuts the door behind him before getting in the front seat, while Isaac begins to reply to Lizzy so she knows he is on his way.

Only his phone dings again.

Opening it up, her newest message reads, "*Isn't our baby the cutest?*"

Right below it is a picture she must've taken with her phone, of her kissing Malik's cheek while he stares straight into the camera, tears streaming down his face, and confirming Isaac's worst fear.

The sight prompts a single thought, one he is sure is completely appropriate in this moment, and that is…

She's a fucking dead woman.

19

SIMONE

"Oh, isn't he just the cutest!"

Turning my head from where I'm looking at outfits for Malik, Helen having just left me to go to the restroom, I discover a woman with long light brown hair bending down in front of my son's stroller sporting a big smile. The grin widens when she looks up to see me watching her, after which she rises from her crouch, holding out her hand as she says, "I must say, he looks like you, but more like his father than anything else."

A small sliver of alarm shoots through me at this woman knowing my son, or me for that matter since I'm sure I've never met her before, but it quickly dissipates after giving her the once over. Although she's thinner and her hair's a different shade, I recognize her as Isaac's ex-fiancée from the pictures on the Internet, when I'd researched him that day in the library. There hadn't been many, but plenty enough I'm sure she's the person standing in front of me, and she confirms it when I finally put my hand in hers.

"Elizabeth Parker," she states, giving my hand a squeeze before dropping it. "And you must be Simone, Isaac's new girlfriend."

Although I don't know why they broke up, she seems rather nice to me, so I decide to remain polite — especially since she knows who I am, which might mean her and Isaac are still in touch.

"Yes, I am. And I don't mean to be rude, but how do you know—"

She laughs, cutting in before I can even finish asking my question, her smile as well as her blue eyes soft and radiant. "How do I know who you are? Why, from Isaac, of course. Him, my father, and I still stay in touch. He adores you, you know, and this little boy of his."

"Ah. Well, Malik does love his father—"

She brings up her hands and clasps them together in front of her chest, interrupting me once again. "Do you think you could help me? I know his birthday is coming up soon and I haven't gotten him a present since we broke up."

I blink at the way she abruptly changes the topic, glancing back over my shoulder toward where Helen walked off to as I reply, "Um, I'm kind of waiting on someone."

"Just for a moment or two. I know you're probably kept busy by him — I remember he always wanted to go and—"

Now it's my turn to interject because I've no desire to hear about her relationship with Isaac no matter how nice she seems, grabbing the handles of the stroller as I lift one brow at her. "Okay, sure, just for a moment. What were you thinking?"

"I found something over this way."

Turning on her heel, she walks toward the men's section, which is upfront and not far from the children's section so I know Helen will find me easily. She starts searching through the rack of shirts with quick flicks of her fingers, and after a moment, her eyes widen when she looks back over at me.

"Oh, is that your friend coming this way?"

Glancing back over my shoulder, I see a woman walking but it isn't Helen, which makes me wonder what's taking her so long. Then, I hear the snap of Malik's seatbelt and jerk my head back around, gasping when I notice it's too late.

The stupid bitch is holding my son in her arms, with a cold look in her eyes, a small gun she must've had hidden in her pocket pointed right at me, and her finger on the trigger.

"I'm going to carry your son out of the store and you're going to walk beside me as if nothing's wrong," she says in a hard tone, nodding toward the front doors, moving the barrel until it's steady against my son's side at the same time. "If you scream or try to get any attention, I will shoot him so fast you won't even have a chance to blink to save his life. Got it?"

Wanting to protect my son, and not knowing what this woman is capable of, I grab the handles of the stroller while stuttering, "Y-yes. Please don't hurt him; he's just a baby."

"Not as long as you do what I say." She inclines her head toward the door again. "Move."

Trying to hold it together and keep my face from showing my anxiety, I begin walking and she falls into step beside me, saying in a deceptively cheerful voice, "You too!" when the attendant tells us to have a nice day. The doors open automatically as we approach, and once we're through them, she stops walking and turns toward me.

"Leave the stroller and get into the car where that man is standing by the curb. Don't try anything funny."

I wouldn't even think to dare of doing anything, since the parking lot is nearly empty from it being so early in the day anyway, and especially once I notice how large the man waiting for me is; even bigger than Isaac and scarier looking. Releasing my tight grasp on the stroller grips, I can't help but swipe at a tear that slips down my cheek as Malik whines from behind me. The man opens the limo door as I approach, not even looking at me, and it's only once I'm inside that I notice a person in the shadows occupies the seat nearest the front separator.

However, I don't get the chance to react to that because the door slams shut, the locks clicking instantly as the car speeds away from the curb, and I realize I'm being separated from my baby. Then I'm screaming Malik's name, crying while pounding against the windows, watching her hold him in her arms as she gets into another car that pulls up, the one I'm in moving further and further away from them by the second.

I don't know when the person across the car moves, but I know it's a man the second his huge hands move around my face from behind. Covering my mouth and nose with one hand, he cuts off my screams with a firm, unyielding pressure while the other wraps around my waist. Clawing at the one over my mouth, I start flailing, trying to hurt him if I can or even get loose while cursing myself for being so stupid, even though I probably couldn't have done anything different without jeopardizing Malik's life.

The man's grip doesn't let up, he doesn't speak, and when the edge of unconsciousness comes to claim me, my last thought as my body goes limp is that I hope this fucker has a death wish, because there's no way Isaac will let him live once he finds me.

20

ISAAC

AFTER TELLING Jim what room Lizzy said she would be in, Isaac has Jim drop him off at the front entrance to the hotel. Jim leaves to go pick up Helen, with plans to come back here and wait for Isaac when this is all over.

Isaac also gave Jim instructions of who to ask for when calling the police in case something goes wrong, because at this moment, he is not sure how the hell Lizzy got ahold of Simone and Malik, or what she's done with Simone, if anything.

She hasn't answered any more of his texts since sending the one of her and Malik, and the fear she has conjured in him is similar to waking up to find her straddling his chest with a knife at his neck all those years ago.

It is no doubt an incredibly stupid move to show up here alone as she told him to, but without knowing anything about what she has done, he believes calling police would be detrimental at this point.

Strolling inside, he presses the up button on the elevator, entering when it finally arrives, and pushes the one labeled 'five.' The ride up is quick, his heart thudding hard and fast when the doors finally open, only to find a large man leaning against the wall across from the elevator. He straightens at the sight of Isaac, his hand automatically moving to rest on the butt of his gun holstered on his left hip, which makes Isaac curse in his head even as he lifts his hands in the air, pausing in the hallway while the doors of the elevator shut behind him.

"I know who you are," the man says the moment Isaac opens his mouth to speak. "She showed me your picture." Stepping away from the wall, he points at the wall with his hand still on his gun until Isaac faces it, allowing the man to frisk him. Of course, he removes the gun Isaac had brought from its holster, and steps back before pointing back at the elevator. "Hit the up button. We have a ways to go."

Realizing the sophistication and planning this must've taken, it's clear to Isaac that Lizzy definitely had help, and this may be more elaborate — and dangerous — than he had thought originally. But, for now, he must go along with it until he knows the extent of the operation and what he's up against. Of course, this also means he's on his own, Jim not even having the right room number or floor, and he highly doubts she put the room in her name. At least the GPS on his phone will let Jim know he's still in the building.

When the elevator arrives — empty just like his luck apparently — the man shoves him in, steps inside, and pushes the button for the top floor, while keeping his gun trained on him the whole time. It's not long before the elevator stops and the man motions for him to get out, saying, "Now, start walking and don't try nothing funny. Suite two-A."

Following the arrows on the wall sign, he heads to the right, keeping his hands at his sides once he reaches the suit, and stops in front of the door.

"Hands up."

The man directs him from behind, poking a gun into Isaac's back at the same time until Isaac lifts a hand, and does as commanded. Once his hands are above his head, the man uses his free hand to slip a key into the slot in the handle, and when the light goes green, presses down on it to open the door.

Poking the gun into Isaac's back, the man pushes him forward, forcing Isaac's hands to drop to prevent the door from smacking him in the face, and he walks until they are inside the room and the door clicks shut behind them both.

Not seeing Simone, Lizzy, or Malik, Isaac's annoyance rises as he snaps, "Where the fuck are they?"

Lizzy breezes into the room from the left, carrying Malik in her arms as she grins at him like she isn't having him held at gunpoint, and exclaims, "There you are! Took you long enough to get here."

Figuring the best way to get what he wants is to stay calm and play along for now, he points a thumb over his shoulder. "How about you call off the bodyguard along with the gun he currently has directed at my back."

"Now, now," she counters with an admonishing look, kissing Malik's cheek with extreme calm while staring at him with her chilly gaze from about ten feet away. "You don't run the show here. I know that's strange for you, so I'll forgive you this time, but don't give me another order kay?"

Refraining from responding, he simply gives a curt nod while examining his son as best he can, his concern for his safety as high as ever even though it is obvious she hasn't harmed Malik in any way. He keeps his gaze focused on his child, wanting to hold him but knowing there is probably zero chance of her handing him her leverage, and a second later sensing the man step back as well as remove the gun from his back, some of the tension in the room dissipating at the same time.

"Please," she says in a soft voice, the pleasantness back in her tone and face as she indicates the chair closer to where she stands with a point of her finger from the hand that cradles Malik's diapered bottom. "Take a seat. We have lots to talk about."

It takes everything he has to remain composed at her unconcerned with what she has done attitude as he walks slowly toward the chair, sitting down at the same time she gives Malik another kiss, this time on the top of his head, before turning her attention to Isaac.

"That woman. What's her name?" She purses her lips for a second, then giggles. "Oh, right. Simone. God, she was so easy to get out of that store just as I knew she would be once I had her kid in my arms. She didn't even see it coming. You know how to pick them, baby, don't you?"

Her words making his skin crawl, he asks the one thing he wants to know more than anything else. "She is not here, is she?"

"God no," she confirms with a disbelieving chuckle, making his heart drop into his stomach, particularly when she cuddles Malik closer to her body and sighs. "Why would she be? I didn't need or want her for anything at all. I have everything I desire right here in this room."

"Where is she, Lizzy?"

Her smile is pure evil, as is the look in her eyes as she straightens her back, and lifts her chin in defiance. "As if I would tell you. Let's just say, the chances of you finding her ever again are quite slim. It's…how was I told to put it? Oh yes, you would know about this, after that whole business of yours I heard about, hm?" Nausea spirals its way through Isaac's body while she strokes Malik's head, his eyes drooping shut as he leans against her shoulder, making it clear her hold is gentle even if the look in her eyes isn't. "That is to say, she'll be assuming a new identity under the harsh hands of the person who now owns her, and not in the fantasy way you did."

Enraged, Isaac jumps to his feet as he says, "You fucking sold her? How the hell would you even know—" His throat tightens up with an emotion he's afraid to acknowledge, which he channels into his fury with Lizzy as he shouts, "You have no idea what the fuck you have just done, do you?"

Malik startles awake, his scream of terror filling the room while the bodyguard rushes forward to grab Isaac before he can go after Lizzy, taking him down to the floor and holding him there with the cocking of his gun against Isaac's head.

"Tie him to the bed," she commands in a disgusted, angry tone. She clutches Malik closer, rubbing his back to calm him even as she glares, threatening Isaac when his narrowed eyes meet her hardened gaze from where he's lying on the floor. "I advise you cooperate unless you want me to hurt him as well. And don't think I won't just because he's a baby; he's not mine, after all."

As Lizzy steps further away, toward the room she came out of when he first arrived, the man keeps the gun on Isaac's head as he says, "Put your hands behind your back slowly."

He does, feeling metal cuffs slap around each wrist at the center of his back, the gun leaving his head at the same time the man lifts himself off Isaac's body. Then, he bends over and grabs Isaac's right arm, guiding him to his feet before leading the way to the room opposite the way Lizzy went with his son, stopping in front of the door at the sound of Lizzy's voice.

"Oh, and Isaac?" He doesn't even acknowledge her, but that doesn't seem to matter as she laughs and says, "I do know exactly what I've done; you nor my father ever should've underestimated me. I let you have your time out, which I might've deserved after that whole knife incident, even knowing you were fucking other women, but then you go and try to replace me with that little stray. Big mistake."

The man pushes Isaac into the room as her door shuts, not even giving him a chance to completely process what she's just said before shoving him face down on the bed. Isaac doesn't fight, knowing there is no point with his hands behind his back and a gun to his head, lying there until the man kicks his leg, barking one word orders at him.

"Crawl."

The bed isn't high, and he knows the man wants him to get on the bed on his own, which he does with relative ease by using his knees. But he isn't fast enough, the asshole hitting him in the middle of his back hard enough to make him collapse the moment he is on top of the bed.

"Over."

He wonders how the fuck he is going to do that without falling off, but the man grabs his elbow and turns him onto his side to assist, moving to the end of the bed once Isaac is on his back in the center as he obviously wanted.

Then, the man chuckles, grabbing Isaac's left ankle while informing him, "The great thing about this hotel is the beds are bolted to the floor. Makes installing and using chains a breeze." He rattles the chain, continuing to chuckle when Isaac attempts to kick him out of pure annoyance, his grip tightening as he places a cuff around his ankle and locks it before moving to the other foot and doing the same. Isaac tests one as the man moves back toward his head, the chain not moving much at all, meaning there is no give to it, and making much noise with it will prove nearly impossible.

He curses at the same time the man turns him over and removes his left arm from the cuff, yanking his arm up until it is chained to the headboard, and repeats on the other side. For a moment, as the man shuffles around the room once done, Isaac thinks he'll leave him like this at any moment, but the man opens the drawer of the nightstand and pulls out a pair of scissors.

Stomach churning, Isaac slams his eyes shut, not even bothering to give this man the satisfaction of saying anything as he starts snipping at his clothing. Not to mention, part of him feels like he deserves this humiliation for not getting Lizzy locked up the first time she went off the wall.

Even worse, now others are in danger because he failed at taking care of Lizzy and her problems just like her father had. Simone is out there, and he has no idea where, yet knowing the chances of her going through a lot worse right now is high… leaving him to hope there is a way for him to extricate himself and Malik from this situation, and get to Simone before it's too late for all of them.

21

SIMONE

WHEN I FIRST WAKE UP, not knowing where I am is disorienting, especially since I'm in a rather lovely and brightly lit bedroom. The bed is soft as well, along with the fluffy comforter covering me, and a swipe of my hand over the smooth sheets has me thinking they are silk or something like it.

However, as I toss the coverings aside and roll to sit on the edge of the bed, something wrapped tight around my throat has me reaching up to touch it while my eyes desperately search the room for a mirror. Not finding one, I explore the band, deciding it is leather based on the texture, with a steel hoop in the front, and the lack of a buckle or lock means this stupid thing can only be removed by cutting through it, making me wonder how the fuck it got put on in the first place.

I hate how it hugs my neck so I can't even get a finger under it, and as I go to step onto the white carpeted floor, I notice the same tight bands around my wrists and ankles, sporting hoops of their own as well. That's also the moment I notice I'm completely fucking naked otherwise.

Stalking over to the window, a quick inspection tells me two things: I'm two floors up, surrounded by nothing but empty lands and trees, and the window isn't designed to fucking open at all. Pissed, and even knowing my next action is probably pointless, I stalk over to the door and turn the knob, finding it locked just as I thought I would.

And that's when I fucking lose it.

Clenching my hands into fists, I bang on the door, screaming, "Hey. Let me the fuck out of here! Who the fuck do you think you are?"

"I wouldn't do that if I were you." The softly spoken words come from inside the room, causing me to whirl around with my fists still in the air, only to lower them at the sight of another woman.

With shortly cropped black hair and bright blue eyes, she's wearing cuffs similar to mine, although there isn't one around her neck, and she isn't nude as I am either. But something in her manner makes it clear she isn't here to hurt me, which is the only reason I lower my arms to my sides and relax.

However, when I take a step toward her, she holds up a hand palm out and shakes her head. "Don't step any closer. Not unless you want to get shocked."

Freezing in place, the first sliver of fear since waking up here creeps up my spine, and makes me feel queasy. "Shocked?"

"The cuffs," she clarifies with a tap on her bare neck. "Depending on your position in the house, coming close or into contact with those on the same charge will get you shocked with electricity. I'm household staff, you aren't, so we have to keep a distance of ten feet or we'll both get hurt."

It's impossible to keep the quiver of outrage from my voice. "Like a…a fucking electric fence for a dog?"

"Yes." She lets out a slight laugh as if amused, but the sound is disdainful to my ears. "It cuts down on any attempts to assist someone in escaping, while your lack of clothing makes you nearly incapable of hiding an object to hurt someone, although the house-wide surveillance curtails both activities as well. So don't try anything because you honestly won't get away with it."

Crossing my arms over my chest, I feel like stating the obvious, which I do while tapping my foot. "I have the feeling you give this speech to every new prisoner who comes into this house. That makes you what? A greeter of naked slaves?"

"Something like that." She turns her head to the right and says in a sudden monotone, "I'm in the room next to you, connected by this door, in order to help you get settled and ease any of your worries. I may come and go to your room as I please, while you may not enter my room at all. And please don't try anything stupid. We'll both get in trouble even if you're the one who attempts something, and since I've been here longer, my punishment will be much harsher."

This is all so bizarre to me; not only is this the second damned time I've been kidnapped — I would think it highly unlikely but here it is fucking having happened to me — but worse is knowing this time I am definitely in danger. And Malik, my precious little boy, out there somewhere with that psycho of a woman, and me unable to help him because I'm trapped in this house, shock-collared like a fucking animal.

However, stupid I am not, acknowledging what the woman's said with a simple nod even as the reality of my situation sinks in, my whole body starting to shake as tears spring to my eyes. Sinking to the floor and hugging my legs close is the only movement I'm able to manage, especially when my weak whimper leads into full out sobs, curling into a ball seconds later.

"You get used to it." Her slightly raised voice pierces through my cries, and the only comfort is that her monotone is gone, and in its place is what sounds like a small bit of empathy for me. "Have your cry, it'll be good for you, but then you have to get up and eat. Breakfast is served in ten minutes, and trust me, you want to eat everything given to you. I'll be back with it when it arrives."

"Wait," I manage to croak out through my tear-clogged throat. "What's your name?"

Her response is quick, harsh, and filled with clear warning. "I don't have one and neither do you. If you need me, knock on the door frame, but don't try to walk through unless you wish to get zapped."

"Okay," I whisper, feeling more than hearing her leave me alone.

Allowing myself to cry for a few minutes longer, I manage to stand up when some of the ache in my chest has loosened enough I don't feel like I'm suffocating, and swipe at my eyes to rid them of their blurriness. This is when I finally take the opportunity to look at my surroundings; not that there's much to look at. The room is pretty bare except for the bed, a tall armoire, and empty bookshelves. Walking over, I find there aren't any clothes, or shelves for that matter, inside the cabinet. Along with no books, it's apparent whoever is keeping me here doesn't want me to have any way to defend myself, nor am I allowed any modesty.

I feel foolish, but in many ways, this isn't anything like what happened with Isaac, and the situation is totally different. I want him, and I want Malik, and I'm so fucking angry while being unable to do anything about it. I have no doubt

Isaac's looking for me, but even if he doesn't find me, the most important thing is that he gets Malik away from that crazy bitch.

How dare she do this to me, to us? I wish I would've doubted her more, but I'm not sure it would've ended any differently even if I had. She knew she had me when she pulled that gun on me, but how had she known about me? I don't believe Isaac still talks to her, yet I truly can't be sure. Worst part is, I hate not knowing anything, and I force myself to take a deep breath to prevent another round of sobbing; after all, it doesn't do any good to cry. I have to keep a clear head and do all I can to get myself out of this.

I'm pulled from my thoughts by the woman clearing her throat. Turning to face her, she simply nods at the table a few feet from the door, where a paper plate and a plastic cup sit.

Retreating into the doorway, she says, "Scrambled eggs, bacon, wheat toast, and orange juice. Eat. I have to watch to make sure you eat it all."

I'm starving, so arguing with her is the last thing on my mind, although a disbelieving laugh slips through my lips when I only see a plastic spoon on the plate to eat with, not to mention the fact it seems I have to stand while eating because there is no chair.

"Wow," I mutter, picking it up and waving it in the air. "No fucking chances taken, huh?"

She doesn't respond to that, but when I lean forward and sniff the food, she's the one chuckling then. "Nobody is going to poison you after all the effort to get you here. Besides, poison is the cowards way of killing someone."

Scoffing, I bring the cup of juice to my lips, sipping it before asking, "How long have you been here?"

"Long enough." Her voice is back to the monotone again. "Stop talking and eat. You'll have more important things to worry about quite soon enough."

Honestly, I get why she's being the way she is, and I'm sure her statement is completely true. If there are cameras everywhere like she says, she's only trying to keep herself out of trouble, and I don't want to get her punished even if I'm just trying to figure this whole thing out.

Remaining silent and making sure to eat all the food as she said to, I turn to face her when finished. "Now what?"

She points at the bed, scurrying across to take the items off the table once I'm far enough away from her, only to freeze in her tracks when there's a single, loud knock on my door.

"End of the bed, on the floor on your knees, face straight forward with eyes lowered," she hisses. "Quickly."

I manage to just make it into the correct position as she disappears through her door, closing it behind her while the one knocked on seconds ago opens. It takes everything in me not to wince at the sound of the door shutting and the lock clicking, my heart beating faster while waiting for whoever has entered the room to come closer.

The strong scent of the spicy and sweet cologne I recognize from the vehicle I'd been made to get into assaults my senses at the same time two shiny black dress shoes definitely belonging to a man come to a halt in front of my downcast eyes.

Waiting for him to say something, anything, is torture, and the longer he goes without speaking, the harder it is for me to keep silent. And the whimper that escapes when he finally places his hand flat on the top of my head is soft and involuntary, baffling me more when he slides it down my hair as if petting me, his fingers combing through the strands until he reaches the end.

My confusion grows when he does ultimately speak, his voice smooth, deep, and kind as he rests his hand on my head again. "I feel you trembling. There is no need to be afraid now."

Of course, his words have the opposite effect, because how can I not be afraid between the way he'd suffocated me, taken me away from my son, and has me wearing an electrified collar?

I want to ask him, but I wouldn't dare. I know better. My time with Isaac may not have been real in hindsight, but I'm very aware of how real this is, and this time, I'm properly afraid. I won't let this man fool me; his kindness is no doubt meant to earn my trust and obedience.

Well, I'll obey him, but there isn't a chance in hell I'll trust him. He doesn't need to know that though.

I incline my head a little to indicate I've heard him, and his fingers squeeze in acknowledgment, after which he says, "Keep your eyes down while you stand up, then turn around and lean over the bed, placing your arms straight out with palms flat on bed, face turned to the right while remaining silent."

My whole body shake with the thought of what he plans to do, freezing me in place even though I know I need to move, and his touch turns violent quick as he fists my hair in his hand, twisting it until he's pulling on my scalp.

"Up," he barks, all trace of kindness stripped from his voice, the command cold and cruel.

It's hard with his grip to keep my eyes down and get up at the same time, but when I manage to he whirls my body around himself and shoves me face down on the bed before releasing his savage grip on my hair. Moving my arms into position while turning my face to the right as he said, my trembling gets worse, especially when I hear him undressing behind me.

"You'll want to do as I bid at once," he states,

his voice deceptively kind once more. "The consequences if you don't aren't pleasant. Here is a small taste."

Stupidly, I expect him to hit me or something, but instead, the sudden zap around my neck and wrists scare the shit out of me, making me scream even though it only lasts for a second.

And that's when he hits me as I thought he would, the hard slap of his hand landing on my ass as he roars, "Silence!"

Terrified, his shout along with the zaps and the smack cause something to snap inside me. I will *not* let someone do this to me again; I'm *not* okay with just being obedient when it's not my decision. So, I appropriately flip the fuck out. Kicking both my legs back with a strong thrust isn't something he expects, causing him to bellow in surprise, and allows me to take the opportunity to roll toward the side and off the bed.

Aware I have nowhere to go, I know he'll make me pay for what I've just done, but I don't care. I have the satisfaction of catching him off guard enough to get away, only when I'm backing toward the wall in preparation for him coming after me, I lift my gaze to look at him and freeze.

If Isaac is darkness, this man is light. Blond hair pulled back into a short ponytail, bright green eyes, and a clean-shaven face adorn a body similar to Isaac's as well. He's muscled, and covered in colorful tattoos from neck to waist and thigh to ankle on the front of him, leaving me no doubt it's mirrored on his backside. Only in this moment I wish I could tell Isaac that whether in the light or the dark, it's the intentions of the person which matter.

And there's nothing good about this man who stands there with his arms hanging at his side, not moving while merely staring at me, his face impassive and eyes hard. When I go to take a step to the side, he lifts his hand with palm out and shows me the small device he's holding.

"You have five-seconds to get back into position, girl."

Quickly deciding I'd rather be shocked than raped, I remain defiant as I softly tell him, "He'll kill you if you touch me."

His thumb moves to the center of the device as his eyes narrow and he asks, "Who?"

"My Master. He will fucking kill you when he finds me—"

The sudden shocks elicit involuntary screams at the same time they immobilize me, making me fall to the floor before they stop, although my body continues to shakes with tremors as I curl into a ball. He bends down beside me, making sure I see him grinning before he lifts his hand, holding up what I quickly realize is a ball gag seconds before he forces my mouth open.

"No more talking." He chuckles, shoving the round ball in my mouth, and securing the strap around my head before grabbing my arms and holding them at the wrist behind my back after shoving me face down on the carpet.

Muted screams emerge from deep inside me when he ties something around my hands to keep them there, uses one arm to roughly bring me onto my knees right there on the floor, while his other hand begins to slip between my legs.

Taking any hope of me getting out of here without being violated away in an instant, and making me pass out from massive anxiety.

22

ISAAC

THE ROOM IS GROWING dark when Isaac awakens, his arms aching from being stuck in their current position, and he stiffens upon realizing there is a warm body snuggled against his.

A super sweet and flowery scent he hasn't ever been able to tolerate surrounds him, Lizzy's head resting in the crook of his shoulder while her arm lays around his stomach as she sleeps, and he can't help his revulsion at the current circumstances he finds himself in.

There's no clock in the room from what he can see, but something tells him it's about ten pm or so, which means Jim is doing one of two things: he is either scouring the whole hotel to locate Lizzy and therefore Isaac, or he has followed the instructions given to him to involve the police. And Simone…fuck. He has to shove aside any concern and terror about where she is or how she is doing because it will only make doing what he has to do right now more difficult than it already will be.

He has to stay calm and in control, which is hard to do when the person he wants to strangle is resting against him as if they are lovers.

"Lizzy," he hisses in a low way, putting force behind the words to demonstrate his anger, and bucking his chest to jostle her. "Wake the fuck up."

She stirs, murmuring before licking her lips, smiling when her eyes finally open and focus on his face. "Hi."

"Do not 'hi' me," he snarls, turning his head so he doesn't have to look at her beautifully deceptive face, even though he knows it's not the tactic he should use if he wants freed. "Get off me. You have no right to touch me; not now, not ever again."

"Tsk, tsk," she says with a giggle, leaning up and running her nails down his chest with a bit of force, the sensation repulsing his heart even as his body spurs to life. "Harsh words from a man who's at my mercy, don't you think?"

"You think you are in charge, Lizzy? Hm?" Turning his face back in her direction as her hand freezes on his chest, he does what he needs to do, before she ends up doing something neither of them will ever be able to change. "As if you were ever in charge. You are being a bad girl, and you want punished. Is that what you hope I will do for you?"

"Yes." The word is a purr, aligning with the predatory gleam in her eyes as she sits up, tossing a leg over his body and moving until she straddles him. "It's been so long; nobody punishes me like you do."

She rubs herself shamelessly against him, and even though the thought fills him with disgust, he knows the only way to get her to do as he wishes is to call to her in the only way she answers to: sexually. And he gets it. Even when they were not good, when it seemed as if their relationship had begun unraveling, in bed had been the one place where their connection never wavered.

So good, he had created his fantasy-fulfilling business to replace the hole left in his bed by her betrayal, once he had broken their engagement and left her for good.

However, he forgave her long ago, even if the ache she left behind has been more reluctant to leave. And now, in his current position, he realizes it won't leave his heart because while he has forgiven her, she has never once sincerely apologized for attempting to kill him.

Jolted out of his thoughts by her movement, his breath hitches in his throat as she shimmies down his body until his dick is in front of her, and with a soft giggle, she wraps her hand tightly around the shaft. His body gives an automatic and equally unwanted thrust into her hand, groaning as his cock stirs to life, and has her whimpering in pleasure as she stares into his eyes.

"I need you," she says in a sultry tone, eyes dilated with a lust she doesn't, and hasn't ever, tried to hide. "And I know you need me. It's been so long, how could you not?"

"I am unable to give you what you want without you freeing me, Lizzy." He grins when she scowls, knowing she can see his smile even in the growing darkness, and turning on the charm he knows she needs is the only way he will persuade her to free him. "I do need you. I was angry, Lizzy, and I am sorry if I hurt you. But you were wrong; you lied to me and I might have died because of it. Is that really what you wanted?"

Her lips wobble, her grip on his cock loosening as she shakes her head. "No. No, I love you. I never wanted to hurt you. I don't know what came over me, but the voices told me to. I never would've on my own, you know that right?" Wetness splashes onto his thighs as she cries, and because he has never known Lizzy to cry, he knows she truly regrets what she had done to him. "I'm sorry, Isaac. Please, let me make it up to you. I need you to punish me. It's the only way we'll be even again after what I've done."

"You have to trust me, Lizzy." The chains rattle as he moves his legs and arms what little he can, making sure to keep his appropriately gentle gaze on her watery ones. "Trust me. Remember I am a man of my word. You need to let me go so I can give you the punishment you deserve, the discipline I know you need."

"Promise me you won't leave," she whispers as she starts to slide off him toward the edge of the bed. "You have to swear."

The words taste bitter as they climb up his throat and leave his mouth, resorting to using his endearment for her to make it more real for her. "I promise, darling. I swear, giving you what you need is all I want to do."

A tense few moments passes, but finally, she slips the rest of the way off the bed, nodding. "Okay. Okay, let me get the key."

"Send the guard into the hallway; your punishment is private and between us. And I am not able to escape with him out there, am I?"

"Right." She beams, looking like the woman he fell in love with all those years ago, and not the mental patient she truly is. "I'll get the key and be right back. Don't go anywhere."

She closes the door behind her as she leaves the room, making it so anything she says to the man is muffled and hard for Isaac to hear, which has him hoping the man won't convince her it's a bad idea for him to exit the suite. When the sound of the main door shutting reaches him, he worries the sigh of relief he lets loose is quite audible, but if she heard it, she doesn't let on upon returning to the room.

As she frees him from the chains — first his wrists, then his ankles — he refrains from any fast movements, choosing instead to sit up slowly and sit on the edge of the bed, while she gets back up on the bed. Rubbing his wrists, he winces at how tender they are from him tugging on the chains, dropping them to the bed in order to appear non-threatening as she moves to straddle his lap.

"You need to get into the correct position." His command is sharp, setting the tone for what is about to happen, as she drops her arms from where they are about to wrap around his neck. "Lie over my lap, Lizzy. Now."

Her lips part, her tongue darting out to lick her bottom one as her eyes dilate in excitement. "It's been so long since I've had a spanking."

"If you wish it to happen at all, you need to do as I say this instant."

She rushes to obey, scrambling off his lap and the bed, bending over his legs with her ass situated perfectly to receive the slap of his hand; she's tall enough her palms are flat against the floor to aid in supporting her position.

Placing his left hand in the center of back, he speculates about how the hell he is going to get himself out of this without them having sex, asking her a question she won't consider out of place in order to stall all he can. "Tell me why you are being punished, darling. And how many slaps I should give you for what you have done, as well as why you have chosen that number."

"Well," she says with a happy giggle, wiggling her ass a little while continuing to stare at the floor, as she remembers is the rule. "I'm a bad girl. I lured you here; I tied you to the bed. It was wrong but I was so mad. And you're mine. You belong to me. I wanted you to remember that."

If her delusions weren't so sad, he would laugh at her attempt to control the situation between them; instead, he remains silent, forcing her to continue with telling him what he's demanded her to say.

"Ten smacks—"

She's cut off by the sound of her guard shouting, the words indistinct as she stiffens in Isaac's lap, jumping off a second later and rushing toward the door. Whatever she hears has her tossing a nasty glare at him over her shoulder followed by her grabbing something off the chair by the door and running out of the room while screaming, "You son of a bitch!"

He does a frantic search of the room, looking around it in hope of finding even a simple pair of shorts to wear, but upon finding nothing after less than a minute, he stalks through the bedroom door to find out what the hell is going on.

Only to see Lizzy wearing a tightly belted robe while standing by the balcony doors with Malik on one hip, and a gun held in her free hand aimed straight at his son's head, right as the main door to the suite bursts open.

23

SIMONE

W HEN I FINALLY COME TO, I'm lying in bed covered up, my mouth no longer occupied by the ball gag, and strangely not feeling pain, although my legs and arms ache a little.

At the jarring reminder of what happened, I sit up straight, my eyes searching the room with complete panic, and an involuntary gasp escapes before I can stop it as I locate him.

He's standing by the window, looking out it with arms crossed while still completely nude, clearly waiting for me to wake up because he turns his head at the sound I've made and meets my gaze.

"I didn't rape you." His statement is matter of fact, his lips flat, and eyes flaring with emotion. "I've no desire to fuck unwilling, nor passed out, women."

Once again, this whole thing bewilders the shit out of me, because I'm damned certain he just had me pinned to the floor not too long ago. My throat, however, is still raw from my screaming earlier; mix that with the fear of him shocking me again and staring at him silently is the only smart choice I can make right now.

He doesn't seem satisfied with that, though, and my reaction to him coming to sit on the edge of the bed is to stumble back toward the headboard until I'm huddled in the corner hugging my knees to my chest.

His next question, asked while watching me with gentle eyes, shocks the hell out of me. "You didn't ask to come here, did you?"

"I…" Gulping, I'm not sure what to say, because I can't be sure this isn't a trick, so I snap my mouth shut again, choosing to merely shake my head in response.

"Joy!" He suddenly shouts, hopping up from the bed looking like he's gonna kill someone, and swipes his pants off the floor as the door toward the woman's room opens.

"Yes?"

The sight of the 'nameless woman' responding to being called Joy, in addition to the naked man standing in the middle of the room shrugging on his pants while totally pissed off, is the moment I get exactly what's happened.

Suddenly, everything makes complete fucking terrible and hilarious sense, leading me to burst into a terrible mixture of laughter and sobs that threaten to choke me.

"Oh god," I hear Joy groan quite loudly while the man begins speaking rapidly in another language.

She switches as well, after which they both go back and forth in their arguing, until I can't take it anymore and yell, "Who the fuck are you people?"

"Get her some clothes," the man snaps at Joy, who runs from the room while he turns back to me, only to rear back as I jump out of bed and start screaming at him.

"Simone! My name is Simone, and I have a child whose been taken by some fucking psycho—"

He cuts in with a sharp laugh. "You mean Lizzy Parker?" At my nod, his brows furrow before both of them rise up again as if he's stunned. "Wait, your name is Simone?"

Throwing my hands up in the air, an absolute tirade flies from my mouth to him because he's the only person around I can yell at. "Who the fuck do you think I am? What is up with taking the word of someone about who is consenting to this sort of thing? You had me on the fucking ground—"

He slices a hand through the air, taking a step forward as he interrupts me. "If you hadn't kicked me, I would've asked the question meant to ascertain your consent without ruining the fantasy. If you had answered incorrectly, I would've stopped immediately." My mouth drops open as he continues in a softer tone with, "She told me you were her friend Sylvia who wanted to indulge in this fantasy. The woman is prepped beforehand, and the game begins the moment the woman enters my car. I assumed you wished to 'play' a little more before giving in, where again, nothing sexual would've happened until you answered the question properly; once I tied you up, I planned to put you on the bed and remove the gag to ask the question. I give you my word I had no idea you were truly terrified until you passed out on me."

It's no doubt insane of me to think he's telling the truth, but sincerity rings in his words, and in his eyes. The same kind Isaac showed me in his actions. So, glancing toward the window where it's now starting to grow dark, I change the topic to ask him, "How long's it been since you took me?"

"A little over twelve hours. And," he hesitates, giving me a nervous smile when I look back at him, sliding his hand into the pockets of his pants. "I'm Owen Chandler, by the way."

Joy returns to the room with clothes right then, rushing over to place the clothes and shoes I wore here on the bed, before turning to walk out of the room once more without even glancing at me.

"Get dressed," he says gently before averting his gaze and pivoting to face the opposite direction. "Then we'll talk a little more, get the cuffs removed, and take you back home."

"I'd like to know why people keep setting me up for this sort of thing," I mutter beneath my breath while reaching for the t-shirt and pulling it over my head, only to find Owen has turned to stare at me once again. "What?"

"Did you say, 'keep setting you up' as in this has happened before?"

"Yes, my ex-husband…it's a long story."

As I slip into my jeans, he asks in a firm yet cautious tone, "Who is Lizzy Parker to you if not your friend?"

Not feeling like answering the question first, I quickly toss it back at him. "Who is she to *you*, Mister Chandler?"

"Mister Chandler was how my father liked to be addressed," he responds with a smirk. "And Lizzy Parker is the ex-fiancée of my father's colleagues' son, who also happens to be my ex-coworker."

In the middle of slipping into my shoes, I freeze and stare at him wide-eyed as I recall Isaac's former career. "You're a stockbroker?"

At that, his brows lift and he frowns for a moment, no doubt trying to gather how I know that, but then he tosses his head back and busts into loud laughter. "That's it!" He throws his hands up in the air when his laughter dies as quickly as it arrived, staring at me with a gleam in his eyes as I finish putting my other shoe on. "You've got your claws in Isaac Toft, haven't you? That's why Lizzy's done this, and she probably hoped he would kick my ass when he found you with me." Then, his frown is back, deepening along with the stormy look on his face. "Is the kid Isaac's?"

"Yes." When he curses, I feel like crying. "She won't hurt him, will she?"

He gives me a look that says he doesn't know without him actually saying it, which only makes my anxiety rise as he puts his shirt back on and snatch up his shoes from the floor.

"Let's go," he says, sitting down on the edge of the bed to put them on before standing up again. "I know where she's at, and I'm betting Isaac's there by now, especially if she lured him in with your son."

"Oh god." After a quick glance around the room, I lift my arms and display my wrists. "Still need to remove these. And where's my jacket? I need my phone—"

"Yes." He holds up a hand to halt the stream of words. "One thing at a time all right? Follow me."

He pivots on his heels and walks toward the door, leaving me with nothing to do except trust him and obey his orders.

The fact I'm obeying him after swearing I wouldn't earlier makes me smile even though I shouldn't, but it's funny what a change in the actual situation will do to promises I make to myself.

And honestly, I'll continue to do what he says as long as he gets me back in one piece to the man I love and our child, along with making sure Lizzy Parker gets what's coming to her for doing this to all of us.

AFTER THE REMOVAL OF THE NOT-SO-TRULY-dangerous cuffs and collar, the return of the rest of my things, and a quick call to both Isaac and Jim's phones which go straight to voicemail while heightening my worry, Owen and I are riding in his car toward the hotel where he says Lizzy is currently staying.

I'm not really sure, even after his answer earlier, why he stays in contact with her. But, honestly, not sure it's any of my business, so that's why I haven't asked for clarification. However, the one thing I'm truly curious about is whether he has any knowledge about Isaac he can share, so I decide to just straight up ask him.

Turning away from where I'm staring out the window on my end of the seat, only to find him staring out his on the other end makes me smile because he doesn't notice me watching him. I'm glad, because in truth, whether I look at him in profile view or straight face-to-face, there is no denying this man is perfect physically. And, although I won't say it out loud, he is attractive to me, which makes me feel guilty because of... well...Isaac.

Not that sex for everyone is intertwined with love, because I know that isn't true at all; however, as far as I understand it, our relationship is defined as sex being between me and Isaac only. I'm curious in spite of that fact, maybe because before Isaac, my experience had been limited to my husband.

Owen turns his head, catching me ogling him, and grins. "Not fair to gaze at a man with lust-filled eyes and not let him have even a taste, especially when he's already seen you in the nude."

My mouth drops open at knowing my thoughts are so transparent. "What?"

He slides closer, making himself comfortable in my personal space, and lifts his left hand to cup my cheek while regarding me with an amorous smile and hooded eyes. "You're a gorgeous woman, and I'm considered a virile, attractive man; it's only natural we're curious about one another. No need to feel ashamed of how your body is drawn to me."

Surrounded by his heat, the warmth of his

touch as well as in his voice, and the sexy subtle scent of his body, he holds me captive in this moment. He doesn't give me an opportunity to respond positively or negatively, his lips descending on my slightly parted ones, not missing a beat before taking it further and claiming the inside of my mouth with his tongue.

For a few seconds, I let him kiss me, not reciprocating in any way. I'm too stunned by the way my body roars to life even after all it's been through today, arousal pooling between my legs from his kiss and the way he strokes my cheek with the pad of his thumb, both his hands holding my head firm and still to aid in his sensual invasion of my mouth.

This is new to me, so new to me, but not even thinking about Isaac keeps my body from responding to him, and in this moment I hate him for having trained me to respond to touch no matter what. And I hate Owen. I hate how my body likes his touch, comes alive for it, even though he isn't the man I love, confirming the two things aren't connected in my mind anymore — not like they used to be when I was married — and probably never will be again thanks to all the bullshit I've been through.

It hurts, and it makes me angry; furious enough to push Owen away with all the strength I have and slap him across the face hard the moment our lips part. The action sufficiently shocks the shit out of us both as his head rears back and his hands drop away from me.

"Wow," he mutters after a moment, rubbing his cheek while both of us stare at one another, breathing hard and fast. When he finally says something, his amusement is unmistakable. "All right. I deserved that."

For some reason, I feel the need to protest, touching the tips of my fingers to my lips. "No. I'm sorry. I—you're right. I love Isaac, but it doesn't stop me from wanting to have sex with you. I...I'm not sure what to feel, and with all this going on—"

"Hey." His voice is sharp, causing us both to wince before his hand returns to face my face, and he strokes it while speaking softer. "Hey. You're lovely, and Isaac is quite the lucky man to have you feel like you do. I shouldn't have given in to the urge; I know better, and he's going to kick my fucking ass for doing so."

Terrible as it is, my face burns as I blurt out, "Don't tell him. Can't...can't we just forget it?"

"Ah. No, sweetheart. I'm afraid everything you feel is written all over your face. He'll know, trust me." Face full of sympathy, he leans in and presses a soft kiss to the corner of my mouth, frowning as he stares over my shoulder, and the car slows down before stopping completely. "We're here."

"Wait," I say quietly as he goes to open the door, placing my hand on his arm while my eyes fill with tears. "Lizzy…Isaac…What happened between them? He never told me, and maybe if he had, this all might've been avoided?"

His reply is low, firm, and reassuring. "Isaac is an honorable man. What happened between them is something he needs to tell you himself, but I can say she betrayed him then, just like she's betrayed his wishes now, of that I have no doubt."

"Were…were you a part of it?"

Heat flares in his eyes, dying just as quick as I'm sure he realizes I'm not trying to insult him, and he states flatly, "No. We were never friends, but neither were we enemies. What happened was private, between them, and made Isaac want out of the life he led; something I can't say I blame him for at all."

"Okay." Wiping away the tears slipping down my cheeks, I take a deep breath and nod. "Okay, I'm ready."

At least, I think I am, until Owen busts into Lizzy's hotel room after taking out her guard, discovering Isaac standing stark naked in the center of the living room while she hovers by the balcony doors with my sobbing son in hand, the gun barrel pointed right at him, and a nasty smirk on her lips.

"Oh look," Lizzy says in a nasty voice while keeping her icy gaze locked to Isaac's troubled one. "Your whore has arrived."

Even if he wants nothing more than to look at Simone and see her in one piece, he doesn't dare look away from Lizzy and the gun she has aimed at his child. Protecting Malik and getting him out of her hands before any harm comes to him is Isaac's sole focus in this moment, and he hopes Simone knows everything about to come out of his mouth is pure deception.

"Why do you believe I care about her?" He squelches the urge to wince at the sound of Simone's sharp intake of breath behind him, aiming all his affection for her toward Lizzy instead in a tender, loving tone. "I care about you and my son. That is it. And right now, you are scaring him. If you love me, why would you want to scare, let alone hurt, my son?"

Her softening eyes dart from him to Malik, then back again as she shakes her head and whispers, "I don't. He's precious, and I wish he were mine."

"Then give him back to his mother, Lizzy. They will leave, and I will stay with you."

"I can't." She hugs him closer to her body, taking a step back through the doors until she's no longer standing inside the suite, her voice rising even as her words wobble with emotion. "You just want to get him away from me so you can go be a family with her. Stop trying to trick me. I'm not stupid."

"I would never call you stupid, Lizzy." Isaac takes a few steps closer, holding his arms out, fearing for both Lizzy and Malik's lives now as his son's sobs turn into miserable whimpers. "And I am not trying to trick you. I promised you I would not leave you; when we were in the bedroom, remember? I do not break promises and you know it, so you need to trust me; hurting my son will not accomplish what you desire."

The hand holding the gun lowers away from Malik's body, her eyes watering as she whispers, "Give me your word. Promise you won't let them put me away."

He doesn't have the power to prevent such a thing, but the only thing that matters in this moment is removing his son from her grasp, so he nods. "We can resolve this between us. There is no need for anyone to get in trouble here, especially when none of us have come to any harm."

"Okay! Okay." Continuing to stare at him in consideration, she nods and says, "Take him and tell her to come get him."

Isaac steps close enough to take Malik as she holds him out, calling out to Simone while remaining focused on Lizzy. "Come take Malik from me and leave the suite, Simone."

He listens as she runs toward him, crying with relief, but he doesn't dare look at her. Pressing a kiss to the top of Malik's head, he simply turns his body and holds his arms out for Simone to take him, which she does without a word before disappearing as fast as she arrived.

And his deep sigh of relief barely passes through his lips when Lizzy steps back toward the balcony's rail, her eyes narrowing with rage as she hisses, "You liar."

The question of what the hell is wrong now is answered by the cock of a gun from somewhere behind him and the words, "Put the gun down ma'am."

He doesn't need to look back to know Jim, and therefore the police, have finally arrived. Quirking a brow, he asks her, "How did I lie, Lizzy? I have been here with you."

"Your fucking henchman. He obviously knew you were here the whole time."

At that, he can't resist a grin. "Did you really

think nobody would know where I went, Lizzy? Foolish."

"You played me, you son of a bitch." She takes one step back, followed by another, and glares when her back is against the railing. "But you didn't fucking know the real room number until you hit the fifth floor. How…?"

"My phone has a tracker on it." He shrugs, wishing she would just put the fucking gun down, so he could get home to Simone and Malik. "Jim's idea, in fact, because he thought something like this might happen. Even if he had no knowledge of where I was in the hotel, all that mattered is knowing I was inside it somewhere."

"Bastard!"

Ignoring her, Isaac finally glances over his shoulder, discovering three cops right inside the doors that lead back into the hotel suite, while Jim and Helen stand further away, and Simone is nowhere in sight thankfully. All three cops have their guns on Lizzy, and when he sees two of their eyes widen, he looks back at Lizzy only to see she's standing up on the ledge, hugging the rail with her legs while the gun hangs at her side.

"Get down, Lizzy. You may think you want to do this, but it is not the answer."

"Y-you think I care? You don't l-love me. I w-won't let them put me away!"

Out of the corner of his eye, Isaac notices the

cop take a small step forward and he begins, "Ma'am—"

She cuts him off with a shout. "Shut up! What are you gonna do, shoot me? Do it!"

"Lizzy, please." Isaac takes a step toward her without thinking, hoping she will respond to him better as he says, "Do not do this. Think of your father. He loves you. You are his world and anything happening to you will devastate him."

"My father," she scoffs, glaring at him with tears streaming down her cheeks. "He keeps me locked up because of you. What kind of life do you think I have now? No career, hardly any friends, spending all my time in that house like a prisoner who can't go anywhere without a babysitter."

Wanting nothing more than to talk her off the ledge, literally and figuratively, he advances another step, pleading, "We will get you help Lizzy, and I will do everything in my power to keep you from being locked up. I have always supported you, even in my anger and hurt; I will not stop now. Just put the gun down. No need to do anything stupid."

"I don't believe you. I never will again!"

He considers the likelihood of him being able to rush forward and grab the gun while making sure she doesn't fall, but his thoughts aren't fast enough.

It's too late as she mouths 'I'm sorry' while

looking straight at him, tears coursing down her cheeks while the hand she's holding the gun in lifts up as if she's going to shoot into the air, and someone slams into Isaac as a gun goes off from his left.

The last sound he hears before he hits the ground is Lizzy's brief cry followed by complete silence seconds later.

THERE ISN'T MUCH SAID ON THE RIDE HOME TWO hours later with Jim and Helen. She has yet to say a word to him as she sits in the passenger part of the car with him, and he can't fault her for it.

Although Jim, upon arrival at the hotel after picking Helen up, had filled in the cops with what he knew of the situation, Isaac's statement — given after he'd put his damn clothes back on — supplied the rest, since Simone and the man she'd been with had also spoken with the police before their arrival in the room.

Yes, his phone has GPS on it, but Jim hadn't known where in the hotel Lizzy's room actually was, since the room hadn't been in her name. He and the cops had been trying to figure that out upon Simone's arrival, the man she was with apparently having been to the room early this morning. Even though only Simone and the man had entered the room after taking down the guard, the others had been waiting in the hallway hoping Lizzy would give up Malik first.

Their plan had worked perfectly, except for the fact Lizzy was now dead, the gunshot having caught her in the shoulder, causing her to fall back and over the balcony before anyone could reach her.

But Isaac knows she lifted that gun on purpose, knowing they would shoot her, and most likely kill her.

In truth, he's devastated, because he hadn't wanted Lizzy to die. She had simply needed help, and although not completely at fault, her father will spend the rest of his life knowing he'd failed to protect his daughter from herself.

As will Isaac.

Blaming himself is the last thing he should be doing right now. After all, he'd had no knowledge of the cops waiting outside, and while impossible to know for sure, he may have been able to get the gun from her if everyone had left them alone, as he'd wanted.

And he wasn't sure how the hell it had gotten to this point or what he could have done differently.

"Sir?"

Dragging his attention from his thoughts and his gaze from the window, Isaac sighs while lifting his eyes to the back of Jim's head in the driver's seat. "Hm?"

"Security informed me Simone and Malik returned safely, and Owen Chandler remains there at Simone's request."

Isaac frowns. "Why does his name sound familiar?"

"You worked at the same company, sir. Also, his father, Bryce Chandler, was a colleague of your father. They worked together during his short time at the University before your father's death."

With only a vague recollection of this man and nothing important about him coming to mind, Isaac turns his next question to something more significant. "Did you disclose my situation with Lizzy to Simone before everything went down this evening?"

"Yes, sir," Jim says, his tone apologetic. "Before going into the room, she demanded to know why exactly these events had occurred. She wasn't pleased, to say the least."

"As she shouldn't be," Helen snaps at him, finally breaking her silence to glare at him from where she sits across from him, her arms over her chest. "You endangered her life and that of her son. You're lucky the man she ended up with wasn't a fucking asshole snake—" She halts in her tirade as her voice breaks with emotion, taking a deep breath before resuming her well-deserved rant. "I'm well aware of how fucking dangerous this woman was and you could've done something about it, yet you let her live her life like her trying to slice your throat was no big deal. Well, Simone deserves better than to be with someone who willingly puts her in danger — not only at the hands of her ex, but now by you as well!"

The car rolls to a stop in front of the house then.

Isaac watches as Jim, after shutting off the car, turns in his seat to say something to Helen, only for her to shake her head at him and say, "Don't you talk to me either. Neither of you say one word to either of us until we're good and damn ready to talk."

She opens the door and climbs out before slamming it behind her, leaving Isaac impressed with her obvious concern about Simone, and Jim unhappy, the frown on his face saying it all.

"Believe there is any chance Simone is not as angry?"

Jim lets out a short bark of laughter. "No. And frankly sir, we both deserve this."

"That is what I thought," he mutters while swinging his door open and steps out, using every step into his house and toward Simone's room considering everything he needs to say to her.

Only to stop short upon entering her room to see her fully dressed, sound asleep on top of the covers, and cuddled up against an equally dozing Owen.

Hurting from the loss of Lizzy — because he

had loved her a lot at one point — as well as the sight of Simone receiving well-deserved comfort from someone who isn't him after the day she's had, he pivots on his heels and leaves the room as quietly as he arrived, shutting the door softly behind him before returning to his own and locking himself inside.

～

THE PHONE CALL TO ALFRED BECOMES THE hardest thing Isaac has to do.

For hours, since retreating to his room, he has been staring at his phone, attempting to force himself to call and talk to Alfred as he knows he should. There is no doubt the cops already called him earlier as he had given them Alfred's number, and perhaps he's already been to the morgue to confirm it's Lizzy's body, mangled from her long fall.

But he wouldn't know the truth, since the police agreed to leave out Isaac and everyone else's part in her ending up on the balcony. He doesn't see it as hiding what happened; rather, protecting and preserving the privacy of those who have been through enough, even if it could have been worse.

Yet, they both have culpability in her death. While he has no desire to cause Alfred more hurt than he is already feeling, the man has to know what his daughter did, and how she ended up falling to her death from the highest balcony in the hotel. Furthermore, how his decisions in regard to her care from the moment he introduced his daughter to Isaac, all the way to her escape, failed Lizzy in every way.

Isaac never requested her seclusion or for her to quit working. He thought her work kept her grounded, even if only a little bit, and having her mostly trapped in her own home had no doubt exacerbated her anger, as well as her delusions.

Dialing Alfred, he holds his breath, mostly in hopes the man is in bed so this discussion can't take place right now, but no. Alfred answers on the third ring, his voice thick with his grief and tears.

"Isaac. I suppose you heard the news."

Having not watched television in a long time — where Isaac's sure they have reported on the death of a once famous actress' apparent suicide by now — he is unable to keep his own guilt and sadness out of his voice. "I am aware of Lizzy's death, Alfred, as I was there when it happened."

Alfred sucks in a sharp breath Isaac can practically feel through the phone. "What? They told me she was alone and had a gun—"

"It is better than the truth, Alfred," he cuts in with a hard edge to his tone, "as your daughter kidnapped my son while trying to permanently get rid of the woman I intend to make my wife, as well as had her henchman tie me up to keep me hostage in her hotel room."

"No!" Alfred's response is filled with anger and disbelief, underlined with despair. "She wouldn't do that! She wasn't that type of person…why would you say that; you're like a son to me…"

"I have no reason to lie to you Alfred, but it is better for the public to believe she committed suicide by cop due to her personal problems, than to have everyone know what she had truly been doing earlier in the day. No matter what she has done, she does not deserve to be remembered for those actions."

As the old man starts weeping on the other end, it is impossible for Isaac not to feel sorry for him, for everything he had been put through with Lizzy after her mother's death. It was the event Alfred has long believed caused his daughter's mental illness — nothing conclusive had ever been decided as to what she suffered from — to fully manifest itself, and no amount of medication seemed to work in regard to treatment. It is in this brief moment Isaac realizes he should say no more because Lizzy's father will suffer for the rest of his life with what she has done on his watch.

Instead, he comforts him in the only way he knows how. "I apologize, Alfred. I wish I had been able to save her. I tried to talk her down, but she said she had no desire to live life like that any longer."

As Alfred calms down and finally speaks, what he says is nothing Isaac expects him to say, his voice cracking the whole time. "Thank you, son. For not ruining what little good her life is known for, for telling me, and mostly, for loving my daughter when you did. I never should've hidden it from you, but when she was with you, she seemed like her old self, and for my own thoughtless reasons I didn't tell you the most important part of her life. And for that, I am sorry, even if it only gave her some happiness for a short while."

He hangs up before Isaac can reply, leaving him to his memories and all the previous times Alfred had apologized, but none of them compare to the apology he just received. It won't take away the hurt Lizzy caused in his life back then or now, yet it is a start.

Something Isaac desperately needs.

Something he will hopefully have with Simone and Malik soon.

SIMONE

My eyes are burning when I finally wake up early the next morning.

They hurt so bad, no doubt from the amount of crying I did last night, it's the first thing I notice; the second is the fact I'm not alone in my bed.

Doesn't take me more than a second to remember everything though, and when I tilt my head back from where it's resting on Owen's chest to look at him he's already awake, smiling at me when our gazes meet.

"I can't believe I fell asleep in your bed," he whispers dramatically. "And am alive the next morning to talk about it at that."

My reply is muttered and irritable as his arm around me tightens. "Who knows if he even came home?"

"Of course he did. He only said that stuff for

Lizzy's benefit to get her to release Malik, and I'm sure you know that."

"I do."

And truly, I get Isaac had put on a show last night, but it doesn't make what I heard any easier to take, especially after finding out about his history with Lizzy from Jim. Plus, who can forget the sight of him standing there completely nude the whole time? How had he even ended up naked?

"However," I continue with a sigh, "he still kept this from me and things could've been so much worse, for all of us. I thought I could trust him—"

"Shh." Lifting his free hand to my hair, he slides his palm across and down, before resting it on my shoulder. "I'm sure you can. Lizzy fooled even me into thinking she was healthy and sane. He probably didn't think there was anything to worry about."

I hear what he's saying, but I'm having trouble believing it. A woman tried to kill him while he was sleeping; love or not, why the hell hadn't he done something about it beyond dumping her? The only small comfort is in knowing Isaac only had contact with her father and not her through the years, mostly to keep tabs on her — or so Jim had said. I'm not really sure I can trust him either since he knew all along as well.

Out loud though, I say, "Yeah, I guess I'll see when we finally talk later."

"You will. Now," he mutters, yawning even as he starts to sit up. "Go back to sleep. It's only six."

"Are you leaving?"

He pauses, looking down at me with a smirk. "I should. As comfortable as this is, I doubt being caught in bed with you will go well for me. I wasn't really planning on dying any time soon."

I know he's right. Not that we did anything wrong to end up like this. After finally getting Malik to sleep about an hour after returning home, I'd been unable to hold the tears back any longer, and Owen hadn't even hesitated in walking over to the bed and pulling me into his arms while I sobbed my eyes out.

Despite the kiss in his car yesterday, he's been a total gentleman every moment since, and even though I'm attracted to him, I wouldn't do anything inappropriate being with Isaac. I'm angry and hurt, but not stupid.

It doesn't mean everything is okay though. At this moment, I'm re-evaluating everything, especially my relationship with Isaac, and the last thing I want is for Isaac to even touch me innocently.

Owen, and everyone else for that matter, can sit here and tell me it was an all act, but what I feel and what I heard are clashing in my head. He asked her why she believed he cares for me, and even with everything that's happened between us, it's the one thing from yesterday I can't get out of my head.

I mean, I thought he cared for me, I've surely thought it to myself many times, and made excuses for his inability to say how he feels for me since I believe he's been trying to show it. But has he really? He's basically claimed me as his own from the moment I was naked and locked up in the room downstairs, and again when he brought me here to live; the second time was my fault though since I let him get away with it.

Truthfully, I don't know if he cares for me, let alone loves me, and if he doesn't…what the hell am I doing here? And why the hell should I stay after yesterday, when something that probably could've been prevented in the first place endangered me and my son's life?

"Take me with you," I blurt out to Owen, my abrupt act of sitting up causing his arms to drop from me, even though he continues to stare at me. The words are absurd as they tumble from my mouth, I know it, but that doesn't stop me. "I don't want to be here."

Snorting with disbelief, he shakes his head while climbing out of the bed, and looks toward the door. "You're upset, I get it. But you don't want that. You need to talk to him, trust me." When I don't reply, he refocuses on me, lifting a brow as he asks, "Why would you want to go with me? I'm not exactly innocent in this, yet you don't seem afraid of me at all."

"I don't know."

The words come out as a wail and I throw my hands up in the air, feeling miserable as I go on to tell him everything involving me and Isaac from the start.

By the end, he's sitting on the bed with wide eyes and a grin as he says, "You're shitting me, right?" After a quick motion of denial from me, he sighs. "I know this is going to end up with me getting my ass kicked, *but* after you talk to him, if you still need somewhere to go, I have plenty of room for you and your son, as well as Helen if she wishes to come along. No strings attached."

It's hard to keep the incredulity out of my voice, but I manage it, clasping my hands together in my lap while gawking at him. "Really?"

"Yes." He holds up a finger, giving me a stern look when I rise to my knees in relief. "I'm serious. Only after you talk to him, and I mean a real, deep conversation, if you still want to leave…well, there is no need for you to end up in the same situation you were before. Doesn't sound healthy for anyone."

I don't know what I'm going to do, but I feel better knowing I won't be stuck here if I truly decide to leave. With a sigh of relief, I cover his hand with mine and say with a little giggle, "Okay. But um, one question."

He glances down at my hand before lifting both brows with curiosity. "Yes?"

"Well, I won't have to see women walking around naked will I?"

At that, his eyes practically dance with naughtiness as he busts out laughing. "No. God, no. Those two rooms are the only place anyone is naked. The rest of my house is rated PG, I promise, with the exception of my bedroom of course."

His words make me blush, something I didn't think was possible for me anymore, and he laughs again while leaning in to press a soft kiss to my cheek. As he pulls back, his eyes are so kind, causing mine to water as I whisper, "Does this make us friends?"

"Absolutely." He pulls his hand from under mine, lifting it to caress my cheek with his thumb, before dropping it with a wink as he stands up one last time. "As long as you're aware that friendship won't prevent me from wishing I could put my mouth all over that delicious body of yours."

My mouth drops open, my face heating even more than it already is, but Malik's sudden cries through the baby monitor interrupt any further conversation. Hopping out of bed, I stride toward the door, opening it just as Owen says, "I'll leave my number with Jim, if you end up needing a ride or something, all right?"

Looking back over my shoulder, I nod at him and smile. "Yes, thank you. For everything."

"Anytime."

And with that, I rush toward my son's room as his crying escalates.

AN HOUR LATER, WHEN I'M SITTING WITH MALIK in the chair and rocking him as he lays on my chest, my heart senses Isaac's arrival before he even speaks, which makes me feel worse than I already do about the thoughts I've been having. I wait for him to say something, yet when he doesn't after a few minutes, a frustrated sigh makes its way out of my mouth.

Keeping my voice low, mainly because Malik is falling asleep and I don't wish to scare him, I don't even bother lifting my gaze to him as I ask, "Aren't you going to say anything?"

"I do not wish to upset you," he replies in an equally hushed tone, the words almost too quiet to hear from where he's standing in the doorway. "Or Malik."

"A bit too late for that, don't you think?"

"Simone—"

"Stop." Lifting my gaze then, the fact he looks as tortured as I feel means nothing to me as I motion toward our son, hurt and unshed tears making my chest tighten painfully. "Look at him, how he clings to me. It took me an hour to get him to sleep last night, because every time he would doze off, if I tried to put him in his bed he would wake up screaming. That is *your* fucking fault."

"I know. There is no excuse—"

It's hard to keep calm, but I manage to do it, practically hissing at him, "No, you're damn right there isn't. I will *never* forget the sight of her holding a gun to his fucking side threatening his life, and you…You can't tell me you didn't know how fucking unstable she was!"

"Even when it happened, things were not that simple, Simone. She was a sick woman who had no idea what she was doing. And up until the moment her father contacted me, three years had passed without one attempt by her to communicate with me." With a weary sigh, he rubs his face before slipping his hands into his pockets, stating flatly, "You need not fear it happening again, as she died not long after you departed last evening."

Not expecting him to say that, I want to make sure I'm not hearing things. "What?"

"She is dead." He states each word forcefully, as if every one is its own sentence, and takes a step toward where I'm sitting. "Not what she desired but once backed into a corner, she would rather die than be put in a psych ward. Which is the exact reason I refrained from pressing charges years ago, as I hoped something like this would never come to pass if she were simply watched over in a more careful manner."

"That's it?" Lowering my eyes to give a pointed glance at our son, I lift it after a moment to glare at him. "And I'm supposed to trust you to take care of us? How in the world can I possibly do that if you can't manage to make hard decisions, perhaps even life-threatening important choices, when it really comes down to it?"

When he flinches yet remains silent, the heaviness in my chest becomes so much worse, and the tears hovering behind my eyes this whole time start to leak out and slip down my cheeks.

"I trusted you, Isaac. After everything that happened, never once did I blame you for what happened, and I let you bring us back into your life without even fighting you much at all. Then, I forgave you hiding the truth from me, because even though I was upset, I understood why you would be fearful of telling me. But this? "Well," I whisper, tossing his earlier words back at him, "things just aren't that simple."

In this moment, his expression makes his misery evident, but nothing compares to mine as Malik whimpers, the terrified sound punctuated by his little hands gripping my shirt even harder and his body twitching.

Cuddling him close, I give voice to the thoughts swirling around in my head since standing in that room last night, watching Lizzy hold my son at gunpoint for the second time in a day. "I don't want to be here with you anymore, Isaac. I'm leaving."

"Simone." He strides toward me, placing his hands on my knees as he kneels in front of me, and eyes filled with an indistinguishable-to-me emotion. "There is no way I can apologize enough to satisfy you, let alone myself, for what happened yesterday. Your anger and hurt is well warranted, but please, there is no need for you to take Malik and leave."

"Yes, there is." I don't look away or try to evade his touch, even though his hands feel like they are burning me where they rest. "My life may not have been much to you, but I didn't need you Isaac. You inserted yourself into my life and you made promises with every action you took, and the way I see it is you broke those promises yesterday."

Whatever he finds with his intense gaze as he searches my face results in resignation filling his, removing his hands from where they touch me and standing up as he suggests, "Use the apartment in the city. I can think of no better use for it than making sure you and Malik are taken care of."

And even though I appreciate his offer, it leaves me feeling empty, as does his easy acceptance of my desire to leave. It only intensifies my belief he doesn't love me or really care beyond the fact he feels responsible for me after everything as well as the fact I'm Malik's mother. Perhaps it's my lack of experience, but saying we don't need to leave isn't the same as wanting us to stay, does it?

"We'll be fine," is my simple response, and after regarding me for a few more seconds, he nods and leaves the room as quietly as he arrived.

Crying seems like such a waste of time, but as I cuddle my son close to me with one arm wrapped around his back, the evidence of my heartache shows in the tears streaming down my face, and my mouth covered with my free hand in an attempt to suppress the loud sobs dying to break free.

I don't succeed, though, and when Helen discovers me like that a short time later, she wraps her arms around me and cries as well.

ISAAC

ISAAC WATCHES her get into a car to leave after buckling Malik in, and he doesn't stop her.

It's been two days since her announcement about leaving; two days in which she spoke not a word to him, despite his multiple attempts to engage her in discussion, with her using Helen to deliver any important information to him instead of telling him herself.

Such as the notice given to him last night about their departure this morning, making sleep elusive enough he spent the evening in his office by himself, wondering how the hell shit had gone so wrong in such a short period of time.

Now he's standing in the doorway to his house feeling more alone than ever, his hands in his pockets to prevent him doing anything stupid at this point, like yanking her from the car and locking her in the room downstairs until she promises him she won't do this to him now or ever again.

Instead, the hand in his left pocket tortures and mocks him, his palm wrapped around the box holding the ring he had planned to propose to her with. If the box could burn him, it would, and fact is, he fucking deserves this.

He doesn't expect Simone to understand, and that is why he's let her walk away.

Their situations don't compare. From the moment he'd taken her, he never hurt her; at least, not intentionally. His knowledge of her had been limited from what the papers signed for the fantasy said to his interactions with her in the dark, and that had been it. They were Master and slave for a time, not engaged and in love nor had their life been in the public eye like he and Lizzy's relationship had been.

Lizzy, even with that knife against his neck on that pivotal night, had been the woman he loved and wanted to marry. No matter what she'd been about to do, he knew her and loved her, and didn't want to hurt her the same way she had hurt him. He protected her, even when she did something unforgivable, because he thought that's what loving someone meant.

Simone doesn't understand that, and how can he blame her, when the first man she married had betrayed her in such an intimate way? Nothing Isaac has done will make up for the deep seed of distrust placed by her idiot of an ex, nor by his *own* failure at being open with her about his past no matter how much he hated discussing it.

Absolutely he fucking deserves this, but he has to give her some time, even if he will hate every second of this separation from her and their son, along with having to recognize he may end up losing her as well. Something he would have to grin and bear while being happy for her because Simone is a loving and loyal woman entitled to receive the same from someone who will cherish her.

Taking a deep breath to counter the crushing misery gathering in his chest, he waits until the car is gone and out of sight without so much as a final glance from her before turning to head back inside to his office.

Once inside he unlocks the safe, pulls the ring from his pocket, and takes one final glance to remind him of what mistakes he needs to fix before offering any woman anything ever again.

Then, placing the ring inside and out of immediate sight, he shuts the safe and locks it before returning to the one thing he does best and never screws up: working.

ALTHOUGH JIM'S ATTEMPTED TO TALK WITH HIM several times about Simone since she left three weeks ago, Isaac told him he didn't want to hear about her life unless she, Malik, or Helen were in danger. However, he hasn't restricted Jim from anything, since it has become obvious he and Helen remain in touch. For him, though, well…he invaded her life and privacy once before; he wouldn't do it again unless it truly was about life and death.

That is, until this moment when he goes to look at his bills as he does every month, and doesn't see any spending from his accounts other than his own expenditures.

Jim materializes moments after Isaac calls for him, walking into the room as if he were simply waiting for summons, which with the way Isaac's been acting lately is quite likely.

Without preamble, he nurtures the growing headache in his forehead with his fingers as he asks, "She is not at the apartment, is she?"

"No, sir. Simone refused your help unequivocally, acquiring an apartment of her own for them to move into."

Isaac lifts his head to stare at Jim, not understanding. "How the hell did she manage that? She has no money, let alone a job."

Jim clears his throat before glancing away. "I believe Mister Chandler assisted her, sir, after she turned down his offer to stay with him until she could get on her feet."

"How charitable of him. Is this man even trustworthy?"

Isaac glares when Jim chuckles, staring at his boss as if he has lost his mind, which perhaps he has. "I've looked into him, sir, and he is a decent person; a do-gooder, not married, and enjoyed a little fun on the side free of charge. Although they weren't friends when you and Miss Parker were together, they struck up a friendship after you broke the engagement." Jim's expression asks 'satisfied?' as he pauses, so Isaac nods for him to continue. "As for his taking an interest in Simone, Helen assures me they are friends only, sir, although she also told me it wasn't — and I quote — 'any of your damn business' at this juncture."

"Do you agree with her?"

Jim seems stunned by the question for a moment, but quickly recovers, shrugging as he gives Isaac the straight answer he's always made clear he desires. "I think you've right to worry about her after everything, but if she doesn't want your help, she isn't required to take it or care what you think about her not utilizing it. Also, if she wishes to move on, or wants to work out the issues with you, that's up to her as well."

"I did what I thought best at the time; we both know there was no deliberate deception on my part."

"That doesn't matter to her, sir." Jim huffs, and for the first time since he's known him, Isaac's fairly sure Jim's frustrated by him. "You're incapable of seeing this from her view, and it will destroy your relationship if you can't understand she feels you directly put her into danger, even if you thought Lizzy was well taken care of and not a harm to anyone any longer."

"I do understand where she is coming from."

"Well, the fact she isn't here speaks volumes about where you stand in her esteem at the moment, doesn't it sir?"

Thinking about the question isn't necessary, since Isaac knows her actions say loud and clear what she thinks about it all, and what the hell is he supposed to do about it? Her anger is justified, and there is no blaming her for feeling that he omitted important information, because he had.

It isn't possible to undo any of it, dwelling upon it is useless, and for the first time in his life, he has no idea what to do in a situation like this; for the first time in his life, he's unprepared for something. Losing her permanently, however, is the last thing he wants to have happen.

He makes a decision he hopes he doesn't regret.

"Give me her address." Catching the skepticism in Jim's face, which he is sure he deserves after fucking everything up as he has, he acknowledges it with a nod, swearing, "I want to make sure she is safe myself, and that she stays that way. I will not impose on her against her wishes; I have done enough of that already."

But, for the first time in his life, Isaac's words to Jim are a lie.

Knowing he would disapprove, he waits until everyone in the household, including Jim, is in bed for the night to act on his plan.

He's going to visit her in the way he knows they both understand, and whether she knows it or not, one they both need as well.

In the complete and utter honesty of darkness.

27

SIMONE

THE SOFT CLICK of the patio doors as I lie in bed doesn't frighten me because I've known from the moment I left this day would come.

Honestly, it's impressive that it took three weeks for Isaac to show up at my apartment, and the fact it's in the dark doesn't surprise me either. I know Jim's had my address this whole time, and as Isaac approaches the bed quietly, I'm sure he's finally here because he noticed I'm not relying on him to live my life in any capacity.

The fact Owen helped me start out is irrelevant; Isaac's pride is what this little visit is about, of that I'm positive.

Rolling over is slow and deliberate, with him pausing in his stride as I softly recognize his presence. "Hello Isaac."

"*Min elskede.*" His immediate reply is affectionate yet equally cautious at the same time as he continues to stand in place, studying me through the near pitch black of the room.

I want to tell him not to call me that, especially since I looked up the definition only to discover it means 'my love,' and there's no way I believe he loves me at all. But I won't say anything because I don't want to argue with him, not tonight, when we both know what he's come for.

It's because I love him, and miss his touch with everything in me even though I'm so angry with him, that I won't tell him no. I won't deny his touch when I'm craving it so much it hurts. He can have my body tonight, but my heart is locked up as best as I can make it; I haven't decided if he deserves that at all.

"Don't talk," I say out loud, patting the empty space next to me. "Unless it's about sex or dirty talk, I don't want to hear it."

His response is incredulous. "You are prohibiting me from speaking of anything important?"

"Yes."

For a moment, when he continues to stand there doing nothing except staring at me, I wonder if he thinks what he wants to say matters more than me not wanting to hear it. And when he finally moves to take off his clothing, I withhold a sigh of relief that he won't ruin this moment for either of us, only letting it free when he climbs in and stretches out beside me.

He instantly moves to draw me toward him until I'm wrapped in his arms, his body spooning mine, and his lips press softly against the side of my neck. The position lets him use his left one to cup a breast over my silk nightgown, pinching and teasing the nipple with two fingers, while his right arm slips between my legs, penetrating my bare pussy with ease considering my naturally heightened state of arousal whenever he's around.

"Tell me your specific demands for this encounter," he whispers with amusement into my ear, "since I am not allowed to speak as I wish. By your own choice, I am not your Master tonight; merely your lover."

I hadn't expected him to give me complete control but I certainly won't turn it down. With that in mind, my smile is naughty even though he can't see it as I say, "In that case, you should lay on your back so I can keep your mouth busy."

With nothing more than a sharp intake of breath, he complies while removing his hands from my body, lying flat on his back as I sit up and move to straddle his hips, which has the added effect of his stiff cock rubbing against my ass. He lifts his hands and places them on my exposed thighs, but before he can take command of this position, I make my way up his torso, grabbing the headboard with both hands when it's close enough, and hovering my lower body just out of reach of his mouth.

"You have to ask nicely," I instruct him, giggling as his hands tighten on my thighs at my words. "Beg me."

"You are pushing your luck."

"Are you refusing?"

"Yes." His flexes his grip, laughing while tugging me toward his mouth despite my resistance. "I have never begged for anything, and I will not start now. However, I will make sure you enjoy every second of it."

At that he pulls me down onto his face, the heat of his breath against me quickly replaced by that of his lips and tongue, licking as if he missed me, making every inch of my body sing with the pure amazing sensation he's always made me feel. He moves a little, flicks his tongue over my clit in a torturous, leisurely fashion, no doubt meant to show me how in charge he is of my pleasure like this. It's impossible to keep my orgasm at bay when he gives my clit a hard suck along with just a light graze of his teeth, my whole body shaking as I bite down on my lip to keep quiet.

His hold keeps me in place, even though I want to escape since the sensitivity doesn't go well with him continuing to use his mouth, and it's all I can do to let him know.

"Oh god, you made your point," I gasp, wiggling my body what little it will move to try and escape his hold. "Definitely enjoyed that."

With a final lick, his mouth leaves me at the

same time my legs are liberated from his grasp, only for him to wrap those arms around my waist instead before rolling me onto my back. My legs, already spread from where I straddled him, circle his waist automatically as both of his come to land by my head since his whole body pins mine down, and his mouth descends on mine with no warning. Grinding his cock against my pussy to tease me, his tongue makes its way past my lips, resulting in slow and deep french kissing that I'm sure would leave me breathless if it weren't already stealing it all.

Holding onto him with my hands on his shoulders, I rock my lower body up into his just as he moves a bit downward, making our bodies line up perfectly. With one hard thrust, his groan meets the gasp released from the back my throat at the same time his cock's fully sheathed inside me. If I were able to speak, I know an 'oh fuck' would've been said because my body, while always quick to arousal, still has to adjust every time to his size.

My fingers claw into him, but as always, he's in harmony with me when we're like this.

Drawing his lips away, he pleads against mine because now I'm at his mercy and he can make me listen. "Forgive me, Simone. You do not trust me, and perhaps I deserve that due to my failure in protecting you and our son, but if nothing else tonight you must believe this: I treasure both of you. Not having you or Malik with me permanently is something I am finding quite to my displeasure, *min elskede*."

Loosening my grip on his shoulders as tears threaten to make themselves known, I slap my hands back down in frustration, shaking my head quickly before glaring at him even though I know he can barely see me. I don't want to talk about this, and same as the day I left, I want him to feel bad. He should be hating us not being there, should be experiencing what it's like to have neither of us in his life, as we would've been if that woman had accomplished the unthinkable.

Forgive him? Not possible; at least not now, not tonight, not while he's distracting me with his smell, taste, and touch.

"Don't," I whisper through the tears now escaping and slipping down my cheeks, thrusting my hips to indicate I want him to start moving. "Don't ruin this."

After lowering his head to the crook of my neck, I feel him nod while drawing his cock close to complete withdrawal, and he finds a tender piece of skin to nip at the same time he shoves forward. He does it again, and again, each time moving to another part of my sensitive neck to bite and suck at it, marking me in every way he's able to in this moment.

There's only one word for what this is, mating in its purest and truest form. My legs around him, my nails digging into his shoulders as an anchor, his scent and my scent mingling around both of us while he covers me completely. Every movement in and out is slow, sweet, hard, and deep, etching my feelings for him deep in my heart in a way I fear I'll never shake.

When it's over, when we're as close as can be while he climaxes and his mouth captures mine, the vibrations of his pleasure and pain mirror my own while we cling to one another. And what is most likely seconds drags like minutes before he pulls away from me with marked reluctance and a final kiss on the lips, his hot body leaving mine begging for his warmth as he takes the spot beside me on the bed once more.

Letting both of us catch our breaths, silence saturates the room while we both lie here, yet it doesn't last long because he reaches between us to take my hand in his. Tugging mine from his with the same speed he captured it, I turn away from him, and tell him the one thing I know he was hoping not to hear after that.

"You can't come here anymore."

He rests his hand on my shoulder. "Simone—"

Shrugging to make him move his hand, I remain silent until he removes it, and then say, "I meant what I said before. This part between us, it's always been wonderful, but everything else isn't. Not now, and maybe not ever. And I...I can't pretend. I need you to just not say anything else and please, go."

The mattress beneath me moves under his weight when he leans in to place a kiss on the side of my upper arm, his following sigh heavy with resignation as he pulls away and leaves the bed using the opposite side from where I'm at.

When he walks into my field of vision, I slam my eyes shut, holding onto my righteous anger and hurt at everything like it's armor, so I won't change my mind at a time I need to resist the way we're inevitably drawn to one another. He dresses in complete silence, and I only know he's done dressing by the fact he opens the doors, which is when I open my eyes to stare at his silhouette for what may very well be the last time.

As he steps through to leave the way he arrived earlier, I swear he whispers something before shutting them, but not being certain makes me wonder if it was just me hoping he would say he loves me. A declaration of love alone won't be enough, however; he needs to say it to my face and include an apology with it. Without it, there is no us, and we have no future, and honestly, I don't want to wait any longer on something I know will most likely never happen.

My last thought before picking up the phone while my silent tears turn into sobs is a resolute one: this moment is the one I stop waiting to hear what I want to hear from him, and move on with my life to better it for me and my son in a way no one else truly can.

No matter how much my heart aches for him to come back and force me to never let him go.

"GLAD TO SEE YOU'RE FEELING BETTER," OWEN says as he walks by where I'm sitting at the table, stopping to press a kiss on the top of my head before heading into the kitchen. "I was beginning to truly worry about you."

"No need," I assure him with a soft laugh, twirling some spaghetti on my spoon and blowing on it as he returns with a plate of his own. "I've never felt better, thank god."

He takes a seat across from me, rolling his eyes while picking up the napkin and setting his plate down. "At least when you lie to yourself, and therefore me, you're consistent."

Shoving the pasta into my mouth keeps me from replying, even if he's correct, which he might be.

It's been three months since the night Isaac came to my room, where I told him to never do it again with a sad and aching heart after having sex with him. Twelve long weeks where we haven't so much as laid eyes on one another, Helen willingly going back and forth between our places so Malik can spend time with his father, and where I've done everything I can to keep myself busy at the same time.

Mainly keeping occupied by choosing to enroll at the local university, and getting to stay at home by taking all online classes so I never miss a moment with Malik when he's here with me. And when he and Helen are gone to Isaac's, Owen comes to keep me company, as a friend only. I know he wishes and hopes that will change, but he's a complete gentleman, and I appreciate the fact he doesn't even try to do anything except spend time with me.

I honestly don't know how I'll ever repay his help. While I think it surprised him when I turned down his housing offer, the second he knew I would have to find a job and a place of my own fast, he requested I let him help me with that so I could go back to school like I should to improve my situation long-term. It has become the best course of action I could've chosen, even if I miss Isaac with every single part of me.

"I'm not lying," I reply after swallowing my food, lifting my brow and beaming at him while misinterpreting his worry deliberately. "I think I had a stomach bug or something."

As always, he takes it in stride, mirroring my expression with a wry grin of his own. "Whatever. Glad to see you eating like you're starving again, at least."

"You never go through times where you don't want to eat much?"

"Look at me." He twirls a gigantic ball of spaghetti around his fork and holds it up with a grin while using his other hand to indicate his built and toned form. "I eat and bulk up, and am completely healthy. I love and enjoy food in general. So, no."

Watching him shove the food into his mouth without making a mess makes me laugh and roll my eyes at him. "How awesome for you that your body doesn't hate you like mine does."

"Well," he says between bites, his gaze heating as he smirks at me. "I love your body and that's all that matters."

Every time he compliments me in any way, I remember his words that morning in the bedroom we'd both fallen asleep in — the one I'd been using before things had started to go well with Isaac — and I know if sex is what I suddenly desired, there's no doubt he'll happily oblige. It would be foolish to think he hasn't been aching to see me naked again since that day in his house, and while I'll admit I'm many things, a fool isn't one of them anymore.

Owen jolts me out of my thoughts with a muttered, "What did I tell you about looking at me like that?"

"Not to do it because you'll have to imagine me as a man?"

He aims a grin of pure amusement at me. "Impossible."

"Yes, you are."

He winks, ceasing to respond as he goes back to eating, so I sigh and do the same. When we're both finished, he stands up and walks over to take my plate, walking away as he suggests, "Why don't you go pick out a movie to watch while I wash the dishes?"

"I can do them—"

He stops in the kitchen entryway and tosses a glance at me over his shoulder. "Didn't your mother ever tell you to never say no to a man who offers to do the dishes?"

"My mother never taught me about boys, let alone men," I retort, shoving back my chair while standing up, and glaring at him. "Both she and my father were narcissistic assholes who only managed to attend my wedding because I told them I'd never speak to them again if they didn't attend or behave themselves once there. So, they showed up with a gift, but brought their problems with them to my dry wedding by sneaking in alcohol."

"I see." Walking over to the sink, he looks up at me while turning the water on, made possible by the counter with the raised back being the only 'wall' between the kitchen and the dining room. "That's why you married so young then. Escape."

Since he already knows the whole story with

my ex, I simply reply, "Yes, and because I thought it was love."

He nods in complete understanding, saying, "Go. Pick a movie. I'll be there in a few minutes."

"You're too bossy," I say while turning on my heel toward the living room.

He yells after me, "And you're too fucking stubborn, woman!"

Laughing loud to make sure he hears me, and plopping down on the couch upon arrival, I pick up the remote to turn on the TV, loading up Netflix once the screen flickers to life.

I'm still scrolling through the titles in Comedy when he sits down beside me, stretching his arm out behind me while sitting close enough our legs touch, and leans in to whisper, "Picked something yet?"

"No, but I'm trying to find something funny yet romantic, just to torture you."

"What?" He chuckles, keeping his mouth close to my left ear while lifting his right hand to rest on my jean-clad thigh. "Pick anything you want, although I'm more likely to watch you than the movie."

Turning my face toward him, he reacts by drawing his head back a bit, and my lips curve up at the corners in a smirk while staring at him with a knowing look. "I can tell you've no interest in watching a movie, especially with how close you are, so tell me what you want exactly."

"I want you," he admits in his usual blunt manner, the hand on my thigh squeezing a little but staying in place. "Yet I can't even attempt to pursue anything until you talk to Isaac, make sure he knows why you rejected him, and perhaps he'll apologize without even being told if he's realized what a dumb-ass he's been."

"No," I say with a shake of my head, ignoring the way my heart thumps at the sound of Isaac's name, and everything he's ever made me feel. The way he still makes me feel, even if I will adamantly deny it if questioned. "I don't need to talk to him."

"Yes, you do."

His insistence makes me angry, because coming to terms with the fact getting over him and moving on is the only way to go hurts enough, and my next words are resolute as I basically hiss at him, "No, I don't. He had multiple chances, he could've shown up any time now to apologize, because he's made it clear before he does what he likes, but he hasn't. And I'm over it. I'm moving on without him, because I have to. I need to."

"You're lying," he mutters while studying my face, which I keep as neutral as possible, only to hitch a breath when his hand starts moving up my thigh and down between my legs only to stop short of blatant intimacy. "If you aren't, prove me wrong."

He's baiting me, and I know it, the cocky lift of his brow mixed with his dare ticking me off. The last thing I need is him telling Isaac how badly I miss and want him, because I could simply tell him myself, but feeling like I shouldn't have to. Why wouldn't he just tell me how he feels and apologize? It's so simple to me, and why should I have to spell it out for him to do it, especially since I believe it will be less meaningful if I have to tell him what to say.

"Okay." Nodding, I lean in until our lips are nearly touching and make my demand. "Kiss me then. What are you waiting for?"

In a flash, he crushes my lips beneath his, his tongue seeking and gaining entrance inside my mouth with very little resistance on my part, and his arms wrap around me to lift me off the couch. Carrying me into the bedroom, he sets me down on my feet, only breaking the kiss to tug my shirt up and over my head before moving to unbutton and remove my jeans. Once I'm completely naked, he places me in the center of the bed and strips out of his own clothing, covering me with his hot and equally nude body before I even know what's happened.

My body is on fire, turned on from the kind of intimate touch it's been craving for so long, yet it's wrong. So wrong my heart feels like it will burst with the fact Isaac is not the one on top of me in this moment. And as Owen looks down at me, every single feeling I possess about this encounter must be written all over my face even as we lie here as close as two people can be without fucking, because he frowns and inclines his head in a gesture of pure understanding and acceptance.

Which of course he understands because he knew all along that when he called my bluff, he would prove his point quickly.

It's only when the pad of his thumb strokes my cheek I realize tears are streaming down them, and my stomach lurches in protest of what I'd just been about to do. Shoving at his shoulders in protest, making it obvious he needs to get off me immediately, a choking sob lodges itself in my throat.

And the moment he rolls off to the side, I jump out of bed and flee to the bathroom, giving into the urge to drop to my knees and throw-up my feelings, because I love Isaac and fear he doesn't love me the same.

Yet even knowing that, he is the only man I want making love to me ever again, leaving me wondering what the hell I'm supposed to do now because I'm going to have to talk to him whether I like it or not.

And that leaves me with only one option, which is to work through the anger I have toward him, so we can be what I desire more than anything else in the world: a family.

28

ISAAC

"You're an idiot."

Isaac lifts his gaze from his desk, quirking a brow at the sight of Owen storming into his office, and sits back in his chair after placing his hands behind his head. "Indeed?"

"Yes." Owen stalks forward from where he stands just inside the door, slamming his hands palm down on the desk, and leans in with a scornful smirk. "Perhaps you'd like details about how Simone and I spent the evening last night?"

Flinching inwardly at the rampant unwanted images of what they could've been doing running through his mind, Isaac keeps his cool as he retorts, "With you having tattoo removal surgery, perhaps?"

Not even a crack of a smile in response. "Again, you're an idiot. And a blind one at that."

"How is leaving Simone alone after her

explicit instructions to basically get the fuck out and stop contacting her make me an idiot?"

"Considering at no point have you apologized to her for your idiocy, she had and continues to have the right to tell you to fuck off. That's how."

"Not true."

"Isn't it?" Owen's brows rise in disbelief as he straightens and steps back from the desk. "The words 'I'm sorry' are ones you've actually said? Or how about — fuck I dunno — actually telling the woman how you feel about her?"

Isaac starts to protest. "I apologized—"

"No, you didn't," Owen cuts in, practically barking the word as he slices his hand through the air. "If you had, we wouldn't be having this fucking conversation."

Frustrated, Isaac sits back up and leans on the desk, clasping his hands together. "Is there a point to this visit, other than your implied gloating?"

Owen's response is clipped and equally annoyed. "Yes. After your little visit three months ago, Simone called me up crying and I went over to keep her company. Since then, she's tried to put you out of her mind and get her life together. She's enrolled in her first year of college—"

"Not intending to be rude." Isaac waves his hand, impatient to hear the point of whatever the man has come to say. "But Helen has told me this."

"Fine. Last night, we had dinner and for the

first time in months, she seemed happy. After, when I told her she needed to talk to you, especially about that night and make sure you understood why she rejected you, give you a chance to apologize without being *told* to, she insisted it wasn't necessary no matter what. That she was over you."

Isaac takes a sharp intake of breath, which Owen ignores as he walks over to the window and looks out, making it so Isaac can't tell if he's lying or not.

"I told her if that was true, then we should have sex, because we both know I find her incredibly fucking attractive, and she feels the same about me."

Isaac's hands curl into fists at his side. "Asshole—"

"Shut up." Turning back from the window, Owen crosses his arms and shakes his head. "You don't get it, do you? She was trying to convince herself so hard she felt nothing for you anymore, I had her completely fucking naked beneath me, seconds away from acting on our mutual attraction. Until she started crying and had me get off her, finally admitting to herself she couldn't do it."

"Thank fuck." Isaac releases the breath he hadn't known he was holding, only to glare at Owen for even putting Simone in that position. "Did she kick your ass out after that?"

"No," he replies with a laugh, eyes gleaming. "She jumped up and ran to the bathroom where she proceeded to puke her guts out before crying about how she didn't know how the hell she was going to raise two children on her own, all because their father doesn't love or care for her."

Indignant, Isaac rises to his feet and begins with, "Of course I—" only to cut off, his eyes widening as he holds up his hand. "Pardon?"

Owen's enjoyment of being the one to tell Isaac this news is evident in his twinkling eyes, which matches the widening smirk on his face. "Yep. Apparently you knocked her up the night you came to her apartment. So, in addition to being a short-sighted moron, well… congratulations, you're going to be a father, again. Now what the fuck are you going to do about it?"

"To start with, I may punch you if you wish to continue insulting me while standing in my house."

Shrugging, Owen drops his arms to his sides and slips his hands into his pant pockets. "I'm attempting to beat you over the head with the proverbial brick hoping you get it so I don't have to utilize a real one."

"Thank you for the information. Now that I am aware of the situation, I will make sure to rectify it immediately."

"How?"

"I have the perfect plan," he assures Owen

with a grin, formulating exactly what he wishes to do in his mind as he says it. "As for you, well you will aid me in executing it for your impertinence."

And for the first time since walking into the room, Isaac has the satisfaction of seeing the man recognize the fact he probably hadn't thought this through all that well.

~

"ARE YOU SURE THEY'RE COMING, SIR?"

Jim's questions follow his latest two minute pacing session, and Isaac laughs, clapping him on the shoulder as he says, "Yes. You should calm down. You would think you were the one about to propose to a woman who is quite angry with you instead of me."

"I am nervous for you. Helen spoke with her earlier today, and said Simone seemed rather sad, even though Malik would return to her tomorrow."

Not necessary for Isaac to say he hopes she will come back home with him tonight for good, but of course the notion of Simone spending these last three days after Owen's visit worried and sad troubles him. He hopes his apology will make her reconsider their relationship, although if she doesn't, the fault will be all his. How absurd to think if he had uttered the words 'I am sorry' sincerely, instead of expecting her to know how remorseful he felt, all of this might have been avoided.

Yet, her absence has solidified how much he loves, and yes, needs her in his life, because until everything with her happened, even the darkness he welcomed had imprisoned him in its grip. He had let it cut him off with the world in every way except the small amount he had let in, and Simone...well, Simone is his light, and losing her isn't an option if he can change her mind about it.

All the more reason to hope tonight is the night she forgives him and they can move forward with their life together.

The ding of the elevator prevents Isaac from responding to Jim, who scurries off to hide in the bedroom until he's needed, while Isaac moves to stand in front of the table — set for dinner for two — sitting in the middle of his apartment.

When a blindfolded Simone steps off the elevator, Owen walks behind her with his hands on her shoulders, guiding her until she's standing ten feet away from Isaac. He watches Owen lean in and whisper something in her ear before kissing the top of her head, squeezing his hands as if to reassure her, and stepping back onto the elevator after nodding at Isaac, disappearing from sight as the doors close seconds later.

She remains silently in place, hands clasped and hanging in front of her body, while he thinks about how to begin to make up for everything he's done to this gorgeous woman, who is everything he has ever wanted. Studying her from head to toe, he thinks even if he had no idea of her pregnancy already, it's obvious in the way her skin glows. Her hair shines as it hangs freely around her face and down her back, making him want to walk over to her and shove his hands into it, simply because it has been too long since he touched her.

"I know you're there, Isaac," she says in a soft, tired voice. "I can practically feel you thinking from here."

Hating the worn out quality of her statement, he responds in an equally kind tone. "Hello, *min elskede*."

She licks her lips before sucking in her bottom one, biting on it in her first show of emotion, and then releases it. "Are you going to make me stand here all night?"

Moving toward her, he loops her arm through his once he reaches her, keeping her blindfold in place as he directs her toward the center of the room. Once there, he stands close to her side, untying the cloth as he says, "I have much to say this evening, but first, there is something I want you to see."

Her eyes round once uncovered, her mouth forming an 'o' in what he hopes is pleasant surprise as she takes in the array of photo canvases lined up in front of the windows. He watches her move from left to right quickly before returning to the left to examine them slower while stepping away from him, walking until she's standing in front of his favorite one at the center.

It is a picture of Isaac and Simone talking before she found out who he was, while she also holds Malik in her arms, who stares at the camera with a drooly smile while his parents only have eyes for each other; eyes which say everything both of them had been holding back at the time.

The photo, when Helen had given it to him, ended up surprising him, especially because he hadn't known Helen had taken it and doubted Simone had either, considering the way she's staring at it in this moment. And all doubt flees from his mind when she turns to him, eyes watering while her clasped hands come up to rest over her heart.

"It's beautiful," she whispers, her dark gaze filled with a pain he feels square in his own chest. "And so are the others."

"They are yours to do with as you wish, although I hope you will choose to hang them in our home."

Her lower lip wobbles, her eyes dropping away from his as she sucks in an uneven breath, but she doesn't try to pull away when he takes her clasped hands into his and brings them to his lips. After kissing her knuckles softly, he lowers their hands between their bodies, and decides to break from his plans to eat dinner first in order to do the most important thing first.

"Look at me, Simone," he instructs her, waiting until she does as he says with a small defiant tilt of her chin along with it, and holds back a grin at seeing her spirit is alive and kicking just as he likes it. "Thank you. I know I have done much to lower your ability to trust or even respect me, but I appreciate the fact you are willing to listen to me considering how things have been."

"You're welcome," is the only thing she whispers, yet it's all he needs before continuing.

"I want to say I am sorry. I regret not sharing certain aspects of my previous life with you. Although not informing you was an attempt to put the past behind me and keep the information from the public view, I should have considered Lizzy's level of obsession with me even while we were dating, and acted in accordance with what might happen, rather than trusting her father to deal with everything competently when I walked away."

Simone's eyes slam shut, a tear escaping as she sniffles, taking a deep breath and letting it out slowly. "She separated me from my son by holding a gun to him. She could've hurt me or him or both of us, and I was s-so afraid…"

"And I never would have forgiven myself if that had come to pass, *min elskede*," he tells her fiercely. "I meant what I said in your room that night. You and Malik are everything to me, and I shall do whatever it takes to prove how much I care for both of you if you will give me the opportunity to do so."

When she hangs her head a little, he fears she will pull away and tell him to fuck off, but then she lifts it until she's staring at him, the look in her gaze open and soft in a way he hasn't witnessed from her in a while. "Just Malik and me?"

Although he expected her to say something, it wasn't that, and for a moment he's confused. "Pardon?"

"I know Owen told you," she says with a gentle roll of her eyes, tugging her right hand free to rest it against her stomach. "I know this is all because he told you about the pregnancy, isn't it?"

"No." She startles, perhaps at the unintended harshness of the word, and he clasps her hand tighter between his while gentling his tone once more. "That is, yes, he informed me of the situation. However, I would have—"

"Isaac," she cuts in with a snicker, taking a step closer and lifting her hand to his face. "It's okay. I'm just teasing you."

"I am sure I deserve your anger more than your teasing. After all, I have knocked you up twice without your advance permission."

At that, her laughter is loud and happy, a smile remaining on her face even as it dies down. "Babies are a blessing, Isaac, and I'm not angry at all. Before I arrived here, Owen told me exactly where we were going, although he didn't ruin any of your surprise."

Isaac's sigh of relief is palpable as he releases his grip on her hand, drawing her into his arms and wrapping them around her as he whispers into her ear. "I am glad you are no longer angry, *min elskede*, because I have something else to say."

He kisses the spot beneath her ear and draws away, snagging up her left hand again with his right one while slipping his left into the pocket of his suit pants to pull out the ring box. Dropping to one knee, he watches as her whole face lights up with happiness, going well with the glow of her pregnancy, and he says the words he has been waiting to use in this moment.

"I love you, Simone. I want you in my life, as well as Malik, the baby on the way, and any other children you will have with me. I desire you as a friend, a lover, and the mother of all my children. And your Master, if you still wish to bestow that honor upon me in our private moments. But first, the main question is, will you accept the most important role in my life, as that of my wife?"

When she bursts into full on sobs, Isaac isn't sure if it's what he said or because she doesn't want to, but he stands up and holds her close to him once again, comforting her as best he can. Understanding her emotions are volatile due to her pregnancy and the way things have been, he pulls his handkerchief out of his pocket, and gives it to her when she finally lifts her head from his shoulder.

She wipes her weepy eyes, gives him a tearful smile, and says, "I'm sorry, too. For putting us all through this. I know you didn't keep it from me to hurt me, but I guess I was just so fucking scared for Malik, I panicked and wanted to protect both of us even if it meant I had to get away from you."

"I understand." He wipes a tear away with his finger and smiles down at her. "I am not glad it happened, but I promise to never keep anything from you again, no matter how much I think I am trying to keep you safe by doing so."

"Thank you." He leans in to capture her lips beneath his, kissing her as he hasn't since the night in her bedroom, and when they pull apart, she beams up at him while holding up her left hand. "My answer is yes, by the way."

"Are you sure you are not forgetting something?"

Her smile turns cheeky, the glint in her eyes playful. "Oh, right, I guess I should tell you I love you too so you don't think I just want you for your body."

With a chuckle, Isaac pulls the princess-cut diamond ring from the box, slipping it onto her finger before lifting her hand to his mouth and kissing the back of it. "Whatever you wish to tell yourself, *min elskede*, as long as you acknowledge your body is shared with me only, as mine is all yours."

She laughs, opening her mouth to reply, only to turn her head to the side at the sound of the door opening from the left.

Helen walks into sight, holding Malik in her arms, and smiles at catching them in each other's arms. "I take it everything's good then?"

Malik squeals upon seeing his mother, so Isaac lets her go, watching her walk over to take their son into her arms and cuddle him close. She also lifts the ring into Helen's view, who upon seeing it shoots him a huge smile and a nod of approval before refocusing on what Simone is saying.

As Isaac stands there gazing at what he has now, while imagining everything he will have in the future that's much brighter than it has been in a while, Jim materializes at his side like he always does.

"Everything good, sir?"

"Yes," Isaac tells him with a flashing smile. "Everything is perfect."

It is so perfect that both men hug each other in the brief way men do with the firm slap on each other's back, before they both walk over to the women who changed their lives for the better, joining in on the celebration of them all starting a new chapter in their lives.

Later, when the three of them finally take

pictures as a family, Isaac and Simone once again only have eyes for one another. Their son is captured staring up at his parents this time, sporting the same drooling, yet not-as-toothless grin as last time.

Soon after, the family of three turned into four…and counting.

THE END!

❧

Thanks so much for reading! I hope you enjoyed Simone and Isaac's story. Please consider telling your friends or posting a short review on the site you purchased this book from. Word of mouth is an author's best friend and much appreciated!

❧

Read Owen's story in ***Forever Yours***!